SLALOM

Novels by S. L. Rottman

Hero
Rough Waters
Head above Water
Stetson
Shadow of a Doubt
Slalom

17 Feb 2010

To Kennedy Readers –
Keep reading!
Best,
SL Roth

SLALOM

 **S. L. Rottman**

VIKING

VIKING

Published by Penguin Group

Penguin Young Readers Group, 345 Hudson Street, New York, New York 10014, U.S.A.

Penguin Group (Canada), 10 Alcorn Avenue, Toronto, Ontario, Canada M4V 3B2
(a division of Pearson Penguin Canada Inc.)

Penguin Books Ltd, 80 Strand, London WC2R 0RL, England

Penguin Ireland, 25 St Stephen's Green, Dublin 2, Ireland
(a division of Penguin Books Ltd)

Penguin Group (Australia), 250 Camberwell Road, Camberwell, Victoria 3124,
Australia (a division of Pearson Australia Group Pty Ltd)

Penguin Books India Pvt Ltd, 11 Community Centre, Panchsheel Park,
New Delhi - 110 017, India

Penguin Group (NZ), Cnr Airborne and Rosedale Roads, Albany, Auckland,
New Zealand (a division of Pearson New Zealand Ltd)

Penguin Books (South Africa) (Pty) Ltd, 24 Sturdee Avenue, Rosebank,
Johannesburg 2196, South Africa

First published in 2004 by Viking, a division of Penguin Young Readers Group

1 3 5 7 9 10 8 6 4 2

LIBRARY OF CONGRESS CATALOGING-IN-PUBLICATION DATA
Rottman, S. L.
Slalom / S. L. Rottman.
p. cm.
Summary: Seventeen-year-old Sandro, having always lived in poverty with his
mother in a wealthy ski resort town, finds his life transformed when the father he
has never met suddenly returns and wants to be part of the family.
ISBN 0-670-05913-7 (hardcover)
[1. Skis and skiing—Fiction. 2. Single-parent families—Fiction. 3. Fathers—
Fiction. 4. Family problems—Fiction. 5. Interpersonal relations—Fiction. 6. High
schools—Fiction. 7. Schools—Fiction. 8. Colorado—Fiction.] I. Title.
PZ7.R7534Sl 2004   [Fic]—dc22   2004014585

Printed in U.S.A.   Set in Excelsior   Book design by Nancy Brennan

TO MY FAMILY, *for teaching me that the twists and turns are what make life exciting.*

- - -

Special thanks to SkiDancer2 and Gretchen Nies for skiing knowledge and advice and some early editing help.

- - -

And to Sharyn November, a passionate editor who calls it as she sees it.

- - -

Thank you!

FATE has been known to move mountains—
but is sometimes found buried within them.

SEVENTEEN YEARS AGO

— — —

The day our heroine took her first fall, the sun was shining, and the snow looked more like silver glitter than white powder. It was spring break in Texas, and as a reward for her hard work at school and a potential scholarship to Notre Dame, her parents had treated her and her three best friends to a week of skiing at Borealis in Colorado. Nothing could be more perfect.

She confidently aimed for a small mogul, and laughed with delight as she caught a little air. The next mogul, the one she hadn't seen, proved to be her undoing.

Sappy enough for you? Just wait. It gets better.

She caught a lot of air, and panicked in the middle of it. As a result, she came down hard. When the snow finally settled, she was sprawled on the slope, minus one ski, one pole, and one hat. An initial inventory revealed no great injuries, just several sore spots.

The cheering and laughing from her friends downslope were answered with a wave and an embarrassed grin. She turned to look uphill. Three sidesteps and she was able to retrieve her pole. Then she groaned in frustration when she saw her ski almost twenty feet above her. That was a long way to climb uphill. Maybe someone was coming soon. . . .

And thus enters our hero, swooshing ever so gracefully down. He was dressed in black, from his boots to his ski pants to his thick, curly, black hair that stayed perfect even in the wind. Although she was too far away to see any details, our heroine was awestruck by his grace and beauty. So awestruck, in fact, that she couldn't find her voice to ask him to get her ski, until he was almost on top of it.

Do you believe this drama?

Our hero, of course, recognized a damsel in distress. Without hesitation, he effortlessly scooped up the ski and brought it to her, showering snow around, but not on, her as he stopped just inches away.

"I believe this is yours," he said in an accent she couldn't place.

"Why, yes," she said in her breathless Texas drawl, "it most certainly is. How can I ever repay you?"

I know, I know. It's bad, and the only problem is that it gets worse.

"You could join me for dinner tonight."

"I'd love to," our heroine gushed.

"Perfect," he grinned, revealing teeth as white as the snow. Even though she couldn't see his eyes behind his sunglasses, she was sure that they were twinkling merrily at her.

Too bad her intelligence wasn't twinkling.

Together they skied down to meet her friends. Plans were quickly made for dinner. She felt her stomach sink as he skied away, and wanted desperately to ditch her friends and follow him. She didn't, mostly because he had clearly not invited her to join him for anything other than dinner, but it was hard.

Her friends scolded her for making plans with a complete stranger, and for not including them, but she just marked it up to jealousy. "I'll see if he has any friends he can introduce you to," she said airily, hiding the fact that she didn't even know his name.

Having a hard time believing that she could get a scholarship to Notre Dame? Yeah, me, too.

She quit skiing early and rushed back to the hotel to primp, head full of the romance she was sure to begin that very evening.

At the appointed hour, she was at the restaurant, waiting. She looked good. Good enough that at least two other gentlemen asked if they could buy her a drink. She refused, not even bothering to tell them she was just seventeen.

Fifteen minutes later, she was still alone when her friends walked in.

"What are you doing here?" she snapped at them.

"Just checking on you," they said. "We want to make sure you're okay. Where is he?"

"In the bathroom," our heroine lied. "Now get out of here!"

Don't you just want to slap her?

They tried to argue with her, but she wouldn't listen, and finally they left.

Twenty minutes after that, more than a half-hour late for their date, our hero strides in. His hair was perfect; the expensive and stylish sweater was stretched tightly across his chest. He made no apology. Instead, he merely scanned the restaurant.

"It's very crowded and noisy," he said in a deep, charmingly accented voice. "Why don't we order room service, so we can actually hear ourselves talk."

"I don't know," she said, her friends' caution fresh in her ears.

He took her small hand in his warm, strong one and held her captive with his intense, almost black eyes. "I would really like to get to know you better," he said, accent even stronger than it had been before.

"Where are you from?"

He smiled. "Come with me, and you'll find out."

Still, a shred of reason made her hesitate. He leaned forward.

"You are far too beautiful to be in this smoky, noisy den. You are a flower that deserves its own garden."

I bet you want to puke as much as I do.

She blushed, and followed him to his room. They did, actually, order room service and eat dinner first. And she did finally learn that his name was Alessandro Scarpettarini, and he was from Italy. He was a duke, he said, finishing his education. He was supposed to join his peers in the House when he graduated, but he was toying with the idea of going to the Olympics instead.

"Don't you mean 'training'?" she asked him, eyes shining.

"Well, there will be training, of course, but I have already, how do you say, a spot on team."

"In what?"

"The giant slalom. Is there any other ski event?" he responded, laughing.

Before she could say anything else, he kissed her.

It wasn't until after noon the next day that she left his room. When she returned to her hotel room, she found all her friends in a complete tizzy.

"Tiffany! Are you all right? Where have you been? Tiffany, why didn't you call? We had no idea where to find you!"

She tried to laugh it off. "I'm okay, really. I had the most fantastic night—"

"'Fantastic night'?" they shrieked. "You scared the crap out of us, and all you're going to talk about is having a fantastic night? You could have at least called!"

"You guys sound like my parents!"

"We were just about to call them!"

"Tell me you didn't!" our falling heroine cried.

"Not yet," they admitted.

The fight got ugly, but they were able to calm down and make up. Finally, her friends went skiing, and she tumbled into bed to actually get some sleep.

If you think our heroine has been acting without much thought, hang on.

When her friends returned from skiing, Tiffany was gone. She had left a note for them, explaining that she didn't want them staying up all night worrying again, so she would simply meet them at the airport in four days, when they were scheduled to fly home. Under no circumstances were they to call her parents.

If Alessandro was surprised to see our heroine waiting

by his door with her bags at her feet, he hid it remarkably well.

For the remaining four days, our hero and heroine skied by day, made love by night, and generally had a wonderful time. Tiffany asked for his phone number and address, and although he didn't ask for hers, she gave it to him anyway.

On the day of her departure, she woke up very sad. Her perfect fairy tale was coming to an end. She rolled over and then sat up in shock. Alessandro was gone. All that remained in the room was her stuff, scattered around.

Tiffany tore the place apart, looking for a note from him. Then she went to the hotel lobby and the breakfast café, still wearing the hotel robe. She was unable to believe that he would leave her like this.

Of course he left her like that.

She finally quit looking for him when she just barely had enough time left to make the plane. She hurried through the room, tossing everything in her bags. Grabbing the room key, she gave the room that had given her so much fleeting happiness a last look.

She made it to the plane on time. And all through the airport, she kept looking for Alessandro. Surely, he'd meet her in the airport with a bouquet of roses and declare his undying love, she thought. That would explain why he had left the room so early—to go get the flowers. And then they would live happily-ever-after.

Except this isn't a fairy tale after all.

She wasn't sure if she wanted to tell her friends all the details of her beloved Alessandro or not, but she didn't have to decide. They weren't speaking to her, and had, in fact, asked to move seats so they were no longer sitting together. Tiffany Birch sat alone on the flight from Colorado to Texas, staring out the window with occasional tears slipping down her face, wondering when she would see her true love again.

But wait . . . the best part's yet to come.

Tiffany sent a long letter to her lover, spilling out her heart.

The letter was returned, addressee unknown.

She called the hotel where they had stayed, but there was no record of him there.

Ya think it might have been a fake name?

By now, a month had passed. Tiffany was not only completely depressed; she also had other growing problems on her mind. The credit card bill had arrived, and it included not only the room she had shared with Alessandro but a few hefty bar bills as well. When her father descended on her room, demanding to know why the scholarship applications were still incomplete, she had no defense. She burst into tears and could not be consoled.

You see what's coming, don't you?

Three weeks after that, her mother, worried because Tiffany had a stomach bug that she couldn't seem to shake, dragged her to the doctor, and Tiffany's worst fears were confirmed.

This is definitely not a fairy tale; it is a real sucks-to-be-me story.

"How did this happen?" her father demanded. "You used to be a bright girl, a good girl—"

"Dear," her mother interrupted. She waited until he

had calmed down, and then she turned back to her daughter. "Tiffany, we should meet him soon. If we're going to have a wedding before—"

"Wedding!" her father exploded. "Now I'm expected to pay for a wedding?"

"No," Tiffany said in defeat. "There won't be a wedding."

They both stared at her.

"I can't find him," she sniffled.

"What's this joker's name?" her father growled. He had friends with the Texas Rangers and even a couple in the FBI. He would pull strings and track him down.

"I don't know," Tiffany whispered.

"Excuse me?"

"I don't know his last name," she blubbered. "He told me, but I couldn't pronounce it, and he never wrote it down for me."

Her father then proceeded to use his big black boot to kick her out of the house.

I've never actually met my grandfather, but it seems to me that he should have a big black boot.

With no money and nowhere to go (she didn't want to face the I-told-you-so's from her friends), my mother then followed her previous intelligent actions with a few more.

She decided to return to Borealis and wait for Alessandro to come find her. He was, after all, an Olympic-class downhill skier who came to Borealis every year. She would find someone who knew how to reach him. Barring that, he would certainly be back next year.

After all, everything he's done so far shows how trustworthy and believable he is, right?

So she stayed in Borealis, doing odd jobs when she could and living off handouts when she couldn't. She had a healthy baby boy at the Aurora hospital, and named him Alessandro Junior Birch. (I can't technically be a Junior because I don't have my father's last name, whatever it may actually be.)

It would have been cheaper to live someplace else, but Tiffany was determined to be in Borealis when Alessandro, her true love and soul mate, returned. She worked as much as she could in the following year, and even earned her GED. Two years later, she was old enough to serve drinks and tend bar, and the money started to pick up. Eventually, she and Alessandro Junior moved into some of the low-income housing that lies on the outskirts of town, out of view of the tourists.

"Our hero will return," my mother said every time she told me the story over and over as I grew up. "Heroes always come back."

He's not *my* hero. And I don't want him coming back.

1

"Please, Robert!"

"No."

"Please!"

"No!"

Jade turned her bright eyes to me. "Sandro? Please?"

I didn't have to look to see the mocking stare Robert was giving me. "Yeah, sure," I said.

"You're the best!" She leaned up over the counter and planted a noisy kiss on my cheek. "See ya!" And she rushed out the door, flipping open her cell phone.

In the quiet seconds that followed, I could just make out the radio from the back room, where waxing and repairs were done.

"She owes me one shift already, and she's promised you, what? Three? Four?"

I shrugged. It was probably closer to seven.

"You know she'll never cover your shift," Robert said.

"I know."

"So why do you bail her out every time?"

I shrugged again.

"Sandro? You got a thing for her?"

"Nah. I mean, she's a hottie, but she ain't my type."

"What exactly *is* your type?"

"Someone I can afford," I said, turning toward the row of boots that were waiting to be cleaned and tightened up.

"Man, you are too wrapped up in the money, you know that?"

"Money makes the world spin, Robert. You know that."

"Dude—"

"Let it go," LeMoyne said from the ski rack. "You know how Sandro gets."

Robert did let it go, which made for a peaceful afternoon. Yeah, I covered for Jade a lot, maybe too much, just like I covered for anybody else if I could. It got me money. And it kept me from spending any.

It was hard in Borealis, because you were either rich or poor. There was no in-between. Half the kids at school carried a cell phone, a pager, and some sort of handheld data thing. The rest of us got excited when we could carry an extra candy bar or a pack of cigarettes.

The other bonus in covering for Jade was that she invariably felt guilty and would invite me out to a party with her. I could get in with some rich kids, and while they were drunk or stoned, I could take them for huge amounts of money in poker.

LeMoyne and I had gone to our Friday morning "enrichment" class and were working for the afternoon. The rental shop was only really dead from about one to two thirty on weekdays. Otherwise, we had steady traffic. We had the obvious rush in the morning, with everyone getting fitted; then we had the almost constant flow of adjustments; and then we were back to the rush of returns and the early rentals for the following day. I didn't often get to use the dead time, or "ski hour" as we called it. Our school had extended days Monday through Thursday, so we could have half-day "enrichment programs" on Fridays. At least, that was policy. But we knew it was really so we could all ski.

And right now, we were bracing for the Christmas onslaught. It was only really bad for two weeks, but it started to get busier the week of Thanksgiving and carried through till the week of Martin Luther King Day. Kolton would only schedule high school students for three days a week, but with all the extra shifts I was picking up, I could be working an average of five per week through spring break.

When Kolton came in, he tossed his coat in the office and came right over.

"Go ski," he said, taking the boot from me.

"I'm on the clock."

"And I'm telling you to go ski. I've seen the schedule. You don't ski now, you may not again until January."

"But—"

"Go," Robert said from the counter.

"Go," LeMoyne said.

It was an ambush. I had no choice but to ski.

- - -

The sun was out, and the snow sparkled like glitter instead of white powder. The trees were wearing white capes on all their branches, and there were rabbit prints in the areas that were roped off.

At the top of the lift, I waved to Melissa, who flashed me the peace sign from the warmth of the lift shack. The wind was sharper up here—it always was—but I liked the edge it gave everything. You were on top of the world up here, yet everyone was in a hurry to get down.

I slid to one side, poles tucked under my arm as I adjusted my gloves. Then I bent down to snap my boot buckles. I liked to undo them before getting on the chair lift so my feet wouldn't fall asleep. And I'd learned the hard way—at least three spectacular wipeouts—to remember to rebuckle them before starting down the slope.

As I stood, I heard the excited babble of girls and turned to look at the lift. Four of them were spilling off the quad, looking like poster girls for Ski Bunnies of America. They each had matching outfits: one blue, one black, one red, and one an interesting shade of fuchsia. Without consulting the trail map or stretching after the long ride to the top, they slid off down the right side of the mountain, heading for my favorite run.

I spent several minutes stretching. Although I had done most of my serious stretching, like standing outriggers and lateral stretches, the ride on the lift was more than enough time for my muscles to tighten up again. Once I felt loosened up, I stomped the left ski, then the right, checking the bindings and alignment. I didn't like the way my left boot looked, so I stepped out of the binding and then back in. Locked, loaded, 'n' ready to roll.

My run, my favorite run, consisted of one short blue

intermediate piece, where the grade was small enough and the moguls spread out enough that I could really build speed. From that I went to a short and narrow double diamond that had a steep grade and moguls of various sizes. Then I hit a long diamond, which according to the map was actually two diamonds, with moguls deep enough that I had to really work it hard. I finished off with one long blue, where I could really play with my jumps, and then I was at the bottom of the mountain. In an hour, I could make the run three times, four if the quad lines were less than two minutes long.

I came over the edge of the first hill, and it was mine. I was loose and easy, and the snow, after having the sun on it in the morning, had lost most of its icy edge. I felt like playing, and caught a couple of lone moguls, enjoying the feel of being in the air, but not enough to move into jumping seriously.

I glanced around casually as I crossed the catwalk, the long, easy-grade run that snaked down the mountain for beginners, but I didn't ease up. Since I was the uphill skier, it was my responsibility to slow down, but no one was coming. I had seen a lot of collisions between beginners who were minding their own business and experts who weren't watching where they were going.

Skiing over the lip to the double diamond without looking was a risky rush that I never got enough of. I had no idea if anyone was beneath me, or if the moguls had been carved down or packed up since my last run. But I loved taking it blind.

I caught some air going over that lip, and had to twist

a little to avoid coming down on top of the mogul. I slid right into the crease and began my dance down the short, steep run. We hadn't had enough snow in the last couple of weeks, and I cursed as I felt a rock gouge the bottom of my left ski.

Skiing was expensive, even for us locals. The biggest obstacle was getting equipment. When I was a kid, Mom had literally pulled skis for me out of other people's Goodwill donation piles. When I was a little older, the school would ask students to bring in things they had outgrown and give them to people who couldn't afford much—like me.

I never wanted to work for the resort, so I didn't. Kolton was one of the few independent employers in town. When I started working at the rental shop, I had been able to buy some used equipment really cheap. It was good equipment, but it had been used hard. If I were working for the resort, I'd get a free pass to five mountains. As it was, I could get the local discount ticket, but it was still expensive.

It was funny, because I remember when Mom and I were on welfare, and I even remember a few humiliating times when we had to beg for money in the streets, but somehow we had always skied when I was a kid. We might not have always eaten, but we had always skied. Until Mom dislocated her knee when I was eight. Since then, she's skied maybe twice a year. I tried to use the fact that she doesn't ski as a reason for us to move, but skiing wasn't the reason she had stayed here anyway.

The double diamond was over too quickly, leaving me with the large, too-evenly-spaced moguls of the diamond. I liked it because it was the longest part of my run, but sometimes I wondered if they sent people out at night with measuring sticks to shape the moguls. There were a few places on the hill where I could actually throw an Iron Cross or a helicopter or two. I did more aerials when I was particularly angry about something. That way, the extra adrenaline didn't go to waste.

My knees bounced up and down; my skis slid side to side perfectly. I kept my legs together; they worked as one instead of two. My shoulders faced downhill at all times; the few occasions when I had wiped out in the last few years always occurred right after I looked to one side or the other. The mountain was my personal chunk of ice, and my skis were the knives; I could carve it any way I wanted.

It was a good day, and the quad lines were short. For my fifth and final run, I decided it was time for speed. I tucked down at the top of the mountain, and my muscles were begging to be relieved long before I reached the bottom. I ignored them, just as I ignored the blur of trees at my side. But I never lost control, slowing down and avoiding other skiers easily when necessary. Pulling up outside the shop, I leaned forward and gave my legs the relief they craved.

After a few moments, when I was sure I could walk, I stepped out of my bindings and carried my stuff back to the shop. I had forgotten about the ambush when I left the store; I wasn't expecting another one when I walked back in.

- - -

One of the worst best features of the rental shop was the huge picture window. It was awesome because you had a full view of the bottom half of the slope, and that was exactly why it was so awful. On days when the shop was packed, the customers got really antsy watching everyone else do what they were waiting to do. And on days we'd rather be skiing, it was torture to know it was so close.

I walked in to see LeMoyne, Kolton, and Mr. Risty, our school's new PE teacher and ski coach, talking casually by the register. But they were too casual. Something was up.

"Hey," I said.

"Good run?" LeMoyne asked.

I shrugged. "It was all right."

"Better than being in the shop," Kolton said.

"Well, yeah," I agreed, smiling. "Thanks for lettin' me slip out."

"Was the last run your best one?" Mr. Risty asked.

"Uh—" I laughed uncomfortably. "It was different."

"Different? How?"

"It was for speed," I said shortly.

"Well, think about it. Was it your best run?"

"All my runs were all right."

"Just all right?"

I changed my tactics. "No, actually, it was awesome. It was the best run I've ever done. I can't ski any better or faster than that."

"Bullsh—" LeMoyne started, smothering the rest in a fake sneeze.

I glared at him.

"Sandro, you were takin' it easy up there," Kolton said. "I saw you let up at least twice."

"So?" I shot back. "I went out to have fun, not break my neck."

"Whoa, whoa, whoa, guys!" Mr. Risty held his hands up. "What is going on here? Why all the tension?"

I just glared at Kolton and LeMoyne. LeMoyne avoided looking at me, but Kolton stared back, his dark gaze unreadable, and a small smile tugging at the corners of his lips.

"What is going on?" Mr. Risty asked again.

No one answered him. Finally, he shook his head and said, "Sandro, why haven't you joined the team?"

"Don't want to."

"Why not? You've got a lot of natural talent out there." He glanced at Kolton. "Whether you were just playing around or pushing yourself on that last run, you're good. We could use you."

"No."

"Why not?" Risty pressed.

"I don't play well with others."

"Sandro—" Kolton tried.

"Kolton, don't start!" I interrupted him. "I know you're behind this, and I ain't talkin' to you!"

"Kolton did call me," Mr. Risty said. "And I'm glad he did. Chase and Jason and Bethany and almost everyone else on the team has told me you're good, but I didn't know how good until I saw you today."

I shook my head and started to walk behind the counter.

"You weren't on the team last year, either," Mr. Risty continued. "So I don't think it's the new coach you object to."

LeMoyne had told me all about Mr. Risty. The other kids didn't want a new coach; they all loved the senile one who had finally retired last year. LeMoyne said that Risty was really good. But then again, LeMoyne was dying to get on the team.

"Come on," Mr. Risty urged with a confident grin. "Tell me what it will take for you to join the team."

"Nothin'," I said, and Mr. Risty's grin got even bigger until I continued. "I'm not wasting my time with some stupid club."

"It's more than just a club," he began.

"No."

"You're good. With a little training, some hard work, you could be great. You could—"

"What part of 'no' are you havin' problems with?"

Kolton cut in smoothly. "Sandro's worried about money."

"We have scholarships," Mr. Risty began eagerly.

"Do you need me to spell the word this time? It's only got two letters."

"A scholarship ain't welfare or charity, man," LeMoyne said. "Hell, half the team's on scholarship!"

"Work with me for a year, and you won't be on scholarship anymore," Mr. Risty added eagerly. "You'll have sponsors! And you'll probably be on your way to the Olympics!"

Kolton winced, and LeMoyne put his head down.

"Mr. Risty, Olympic wannabes who live off sponsors are just as bad as people who live off handouts in the street," I said. "I've got a paycheck to earn." I walked to the back room and focused on not hearing anything else they said.

I was able to work in peace for almost twenty minutes.

It was one of the benefits of being known for a short temper; people gave you a lot of time to cool down.

"It could be your ticket out of here."

Okay, so having a short temper didn't carry a lot of weight with Kolton. Flipping a ski over, I said, "It'd only be a ticket to more ski towns, more places where the rich relax and the poor gobble up the crumbs."

"It could be more than that," he said.

"Really? Taking your shot at the Olympics in Salt Lake really got you out of these hills, huh?"

Kolton grinned. "Unlike you, Sandro, I don't want to get out of these 'hills.' But if I had wanted to get out, then yes, taking my shot at the Olympics would have done it. It did, after all, get me enough dough to buy this place."

"No," I corrected, "that came from selling your grin for TV commercials."

Kolton had been the first African American to medal in a downhill ski event. The sponsors loved him.

He shrugged and spread his palms in front of me. "I thought you were the prime believer in the fact that you gotta do what you gotta do." He took a deep breath. "You know, just because your father lied about being an Olympic contender doesn't mean you can't be a legitimate one."

"I'm not *legitimate* in anything," I said.

"Sorry. 'Legitimate' was a bad choice of words."

"I'd say it was pretty perfect."

For a few moments, he let me finish adjusting the binding in peace. Then he told me to go work the register up front.

LeMoyne was busy with a couple of grandparents who were complaining about their boots. I tried to help a mother talk her little girl into wearing the dark-blue rental boots, explaining that we didn't have any pink ones. The little girl didn't care; it was her opinion that a good ski rental shop would, of course, carry pink boots.

When the mother threatened to take the little girl back to the car, it made my day. I had tried being an assistant ski instructor one weekend, and I didn't even make it through the first class. People who think little brats are cute should have their heads examined.

But the mother continued to beg and plead and threaten and bribe the little girl. As far as I could tell, it wasn't going to work. The mother clearly didn't mean anything she said, and the little girl knew it.

When the bells on the front door jingled, I turned away from them, sighing in relief. But when I saw the two girls who were walking in, I almost wanted to go back to the mother and her little brat.

It was the girl in fuchsia and the one in black, half of the group I had seen earlier at the top of the mountain. They were both blond, and both were pretty tan, but I guessed the one in fuchsia was sixteen and the other one had to be at least twenty. The older one was carrying a pole.

"Can I help you?"

Black laughed. "I think I'm beyond all help."

Fuchsia laughed, too. "Well, yeah, but that's not what he meant."

"I dropped my pole."

"Lost and found is—" I started.

"I dropped it from the chair lift."

"Ski patrol could probably—" I tried again.

Fuchsia interrupted, "She dropped it into that creek that runs under the H lift."

"Oh."

Black lifted an eyebrow at me. "You're not getting a lot of points for friendly service here."

I raised an eyebrow back. "I haven't been asked for anything."

Fuchsia sighed in exasperation, "We'd like to rent a pair of poles."

I couldn't resist. "One pair for both of you?"

"I think I'd like to see your manager," Black said icily.

"Meghan!" said Fuchsia.

She tossed her hair. "I'm waiting."

And waiting was clearly something she was not used to doing.

Fuchsia peered up at me, her eyes uncertain.

I glanced at the clock.

"Are we keeping you from something?" Meghan demanded. "Why aren't you getting the manager?" Her voice went up a couple notches.

LeMoyne glanced at me, and I was sure he was glad he was helping the mom and little girl now instead of these princesses. Kolton stuck his head out the back room. "Somebody need me?"

"I need the manager!" Meghan snapped.

"Would you settle for the owner?" he asked.

Her mouth snapped shut, and I caught Fuchsia ducking her head to hide a laugh.

Meghan recovered. "We came in to rent a pair of poles, and all we're getting is attitude!"

"I am so sorry," Kolton said smoothly. "Come with me and I'll get you set up."

Meghan followed Kolton to the other side of the store where the poles were all lined up against the wall.

I glanced over to Fuchsia, surprised that she wasn't going with them. She smiled and gave a little shrug.

"You a native?" I asked.

"Born in Denver. Now I live in Golden." She paused. "How could you tell?"

"You knew the lift and you called it a 'creek' instead of a 'river.'"

"You a ski bum?"

"Nah. Mom settled here."

"I've always wondered what it'd be like to go to Mountain Vista High."

I rolled my eyes. "I'm sure it's just like every other high school in the country. A huge waste of time."

Before she had a chance to respond, Meghan said, "Let's go, Ange!" She might not like my attitude, but she had a pretty serious one herself.

Fuchsia—Ange—smiled at me again, and followed Meghan out the door.

Kolton joined me by the counter. LeMoyne had some-how succeeded in getting the little girl into blue boots and seen the mother and daughter to the door. The shop was silent, and we all glanced at the clock.

"Five till two," LeMoyne said.

"Yep," Kolton agreed.

"You charge her for a half day or full?"

A slow grin lit Kolton's face. "You're joking, right? When babes got money to burn, you let them burn as much as they want."

LeMoyne and I laughed, and Kolton tapped the counter. "She didn't want to look around, she didn't want to talk. . . ." He gave a dramatic sigh. "Ain't my fault she can't read."

We laughed, the flyer saying, "Complimentary rentals from 2 to 3:30 daily," covered by our arms as we all relaxed against the counter.

It was nearing six thirty when we closed up.

"You headin' home?" I asked Kolton as he locked the door.

"Yep."

"Man, you got borin' when you got a girl," LeMoyne said, shaking his head.

"An' just what are you two crazy bachelors gonna do?" Kolton demanded.

I said, "He just thinks you're boring 'cause now you don't do liquor runs for him."

"You need a six-pack or somethin'?"

"Nah, man, I'm fine," LeMoyne said.

"A'aight. See you tomorrow."

"See ya," LeMoyne and I said.

"You didn't need to say that," LeMoyne said as we began to trudge home.

"Consider it payback for Risty," I said.

"Man, you know—"

"Yeah, I do! I know we've talked about it before, and you just don't give up!"

LeMoyne groaned. "You are one stubborn ass, you know that?"

"Yeah. So back off."

"Okay, so you won't do it for yourself. Do it for me, man."

"Excuse me?"

"Do it for me," LeMoyne repeated. "I want somebody to wipe off that self-satisfied smirk that's always on Sirocco's face. Who else but you could do that?"

"Even gettin' that smirk off his face ain't gonna make him less of a jackass."

"Got that right. But it would make it easier to pass his ugly face in the hall."

"LeMoyne, you sound like you got a thing for him."

"No, I'm waiting for that pretty little thing who gave you all that attitude this afternoon."

I was thinking of her friend. "You're breakin' my heart, man."

He gave me a punch in the shoulder. "You know you love me."

"No, man, it's yo' mama I love."

"Don't go sayin' nothin' 'bout my mama now!"

We laughed and then walked in silence for a few moments, but the street around us was full of lively people. The holiday tourists were in town, and after dropping a huge wad of cash on the slopes, they were out to drop more in the cute Victorian town that Borealis worked so hard to maintain.

The shops carried everything, from T-shirts to fudge to Austrian crystal to hemp products. Christmas lights were up almost all season, but my favorite time was the Aurora Festival, when the shops all competed with huge ice sculptures along the street.

There was a large variety of restaurants as well, although I seemed to be the only one who thought it was odd to have seafood specialists in the middle of the Rockies. And I never understood why there was always a line for the Ice Cream Shoppe, even when it was snowing. It was a huge disappointment for me the year that the only fast-food burger joint went out of business. It had been a place I could actually afford once or twice a year.

People milled around us, bright-eyed and excited, laughing and looking forward to their next day on the slopes. LeMoyne and I walked on, hands in pockets, heads down, until we came to the corner where we would part. His parents had moved up here two years ago, tired of the rat race in Denver, and were grappling with the mouse race they found here. They had been in a big house in Denver; here they had a modest one. But at least they had a house to themselves. They weren't in the projects with the rest of us.

"I wish you'd think about the team—"

Tears of frustration came to my eyes, and that pissed me off. "Damn it, LeMoyne, I can't!" I practically shouted.

People looked at us and then just as quickly looked away. A white kid in a patched jacket was yelling at a tall black kid; surely, that was the beginning of trouble.

I tried to control my voice. "I can't. It doesn't matter

what you or I or Kolton or even Risty wants or wishes. . . . *I can't*. I can't stop working. A team scholarship may pay for my travel expenses, but it won't pay for my food. It may buy me a neat team jacket, but it won't buy me underwear. So back off!"

"I'm sorry, man," LeMoyne said awkwardly. "I'm just—"

"I know, I know," I said. LeMoyne had talked Risty into watching him do the timed slalom that was set up on Mount Aurora. He wanted to impress Risty, or at least get some pointers on what to do better. Tryouts for the school team had already been held, and LeMoyne hadn't made it. He was practicing every chance he had now, practically praying for someone to get hurt so there'd be another spot on the team. Making the team was something LeMoyne had been trying to do since he got here.

It made me feel bad, knowing that Risty had offered me a spot, and I hadn't even been trying today.

"I'm sorry," he said again.

"It's all good."

We shook hands, slipped to the knuckle grip, snapped apart, and then tapped fists on top of each other.

"Good luck on your run tomorrow," I said, and I meant it. I really wanted LeMoyne to make the team. He had been down about himself for so long it was beginning to get to me, too.

"Thanks. See you at school on Monday."

We split up, going our different ways to our very different homes.

I hated living in Borealis—it was too expensive and there were too many tourists—but I knew I'd hate it when

I finally left, too. It was beautiful all year long. The mountains—huge, impressive, and impassive as they were, covered with trees and teeming with wildlife—gave me the sense that anything was possible. There was a decent bus system throughout the town and county, and it was free. When it was really cold, I used it. But otherwise, I was never in a big hurry to get home, and I liked the walk.

When Mom turned twenty-one, I was almost three. She got a job as a bartender at the resort itself, and in doing so, qualified for the employee housing. We lived in the dorm for the first two years (not really legal, but it was what she could afford), and then when I was five, we moved into our apartment.

The resort furnishes its apartments with the basics: bed, sofa, TV, table, chairs. The rest is up to the tenants. Even after twelve years, our apartment was still pretty bare. Last time I bothered to count, there were four posters tacked to the wall.

Now, after fourteen years with the resort, Mom was making decent money. She paid the outrageous tuition at the local community college and went to classes when she could. But it seemed like she could never keep her schedule straight, and she'd always end up dropping a class after it was too late for refunds.

When I saw the beat-up Jeep in the parking lot, I hesitated. If I turned around now—

"There are a couple more bags in back," Mom yelled down from the window. "Bring 'em up!"

I groaned but went to the Jeep anyway. It turned out to be my lucky day. She had actually brought home some real groceries. I took a quick scan before I picked them up. Bread, cheese, a bag of prepeeled carrots, a box of cereal, and several boxes of macaroni were in easy view.

At the door, I had to shift the bags to one arm to open it. Mom was sitting on the couch. I set the bags on the counter next to the other ones she had already brought up and started back to my room.

"Hey, hey, hey! How about puttin' those things away?"

I swung around and looked at her. She had a beer in hand and was watching TV. "How long you been home?"

"Fifteen minutes. Why?"

"Put 'em away yourself." I turned and walked into my room.

"Sandro!"

I took my coat off but left my heavy sweatshirt on. Then I picked up *The Catcher in the Rye*, my current English assignment, and took it to my bed.

"Alessandro Junior, you listen when I talk to you!" Mom was standing in the doorway.

"Why?"

"Why? Because I'm your mother, that's why!"

"Not my fault and not your plan," I said.

"I will not take this attitude."

"Fine," I shrugged. "Go back to your TV or romance book and find a better one."

"All I ask for is a little help around here."

"No, you ask that I take care of you."

"What?"

"You've been home for fifteen minutes, sitting on the couch, watching TV, and waiting for me to come home and get the groceries and put 'em away, and then you'd proba-bly like me to fix dinner."

A guilty look crossed her face.

I thumped my book down on the bed. "You really *were* waiting for me to cook dinner, weren't you?"

Mom tried to rally. "I've been working hard all day, keeping a roof over your head—"

"You had a six-hour shift today," I corrected. "I went to school this morning *and then* I worked almost a six-hour shift. And I've been giving you money for rent for more than a year now." I was pleased to see her mouth snap shut and a little color flood her face.

"I work for the company," she sputtered, "and that's the only way we can afford to live here!"

"Yeah," I retorted. "They give you a break in the hous-ing because they know you're screwed!"

"The resort's not that bad."

"No, not if you're just bein' a ski bum for a few years. But to raise a kid here? In company housing? To try to plan for retirement? You get screwed."

"We're not staying here forever," she began.

I shook my head and stood up. If she was really going into this again, I needed reinforcements. I pulled out a cig-arette and lit up.

"Talk about wasting money," she said, coming to stand right in front of me.

I took a long drag and thoughtfully blew my smoke away from her face.

She tried to rip the cigarette from my mouth. With my

extra height, I was able to twist my head away and out of her reach.

"I wish you'd quit," she said.

"I wish we'd move."

"Those things will kill you."

"Oh, and this lifestyle makes me yearn for immortality."

"So what, smart-ass, if we move you'll quit smoking?"

This time I didn't try to blow the smoke away from her. "Something like that."

She coughed and moved away from me. "The school called this morning."

"And you were awake?"

"Your math grade is slipping."

"Are you sure you're remembering correctly?" I asked. Talking to her before she had a shower and two cups of coffee was dangerous because she rarely remembered anything you said.

"You need straight As."

"Only to keep you outta my face."

"To get a scholarship!"

I rolled my eyes. "I don't want to live like a poor boy for another four years."

"You get student loans to make up for what—"

"Yeah, and then I'm in debt for another what? Ten years?"

"Sandro—"

"I'm sick of bein' poor, Mom. I'm gonna graduate and go someplace I can get a real job and make enough money to live life instead of just scraping by."

"College will help you do that!"

"Mom—"

"Sandro, I'm going to help you pay for college, you know that—"

"With what?"

"I'm going to start an account for you and—"

"You've been saying that since I was twelve, Mom. If you haven't started by now, I don't think it's ever gonna happen."

She looked at me for a moment, angry but unable to think of anything to say. "Go smoke outside."

I went back to my bed. "It's freezing out there."

She glared at me. "You can't smoke in bed."

I lifted the ashtray on the nightstand and raised my eyebrows. For several seconds we just locked gazes. Mom had really pretty, pale blue eyes. According to her, I had my father's "dark, smoldering" ones.

Finally, she shook her head. "When he comes back, you'll be happy we stayed."

"He's not coming back, Mom! And even if he does," I flipped open my book, "I won't be here to see it."

I didn't look up when she left my room, and wasn't surprised to hear her keys jingling and the front door slamming shut a few moments later. Stubbing out my cigarette, I closed the book and went to put away the groceries. No point in letting good food go to waste.

I don't know when I first started to realize that Mom lived in a perpetual dream world. It killed me, because she has flashes of brilliance. She got an A in calculus a couple of semesters ago. The kicker was that she missed half the classes, and I never once saw her study. And yet the woman couldn't balance her own checkbook.

That wasn't my biggest problem. The worst part was that I honestly never knew when to believe her. She'd told me about my father so many times that I quit listening to her when I was eight or so. I'd just tune her out every time she started.

But the details, even though they were the same every time, just didn't make sense. If she came from so much money, why was she content to stay here in the projects? And why didn't she have some money to get us started with, like from selling jewelry or a car or something else? A big part of me was pretty sure the whole story was fiction, just like the romance books she liked so much.

It snowed a little bit at night—almost six inches of soft, fluffy flakes. It would be perfect skiing today—except that I had to work. It was almost December, and we would be swamped. I left a note for Mom, reminding her that the rent was due. Notes were the best way to make sure she got something. Forget telling her anything before noon.

As I walked to work, traffic seemed light, but I didn't really pay much attention. LeMoyne was hanging out at the desk, waiting for the lifts to start. It was his big day to impress Risty. Kolton only grumbled at me when I passed him to hang up my coat.

"What's with him?" I asked Robert.

"Big blizzard east of the Divide. The highway's been closed since four."

"Oh." That meant the locals wouldn't be coming up to ski. We'd be dependent on the tourists who were staying up here—and who most likely already had their equipment rented.

"Go on, get out of here," Kolton growled at me and LeMoyne around nine.

"You sure?"

He waved his hand in disgust and headed to his office. He had been lucky enough to buy this place, right on the edge of the mountain and not technically part of the resort. But the resort was putting pressure on him. They wanted his shop. Days like this, he got understandably touchy, and it was better for me to get out of his hair so my big mouth wouldn't get me in trouble.

LeMoyne and I headed out. The mountain was quiet enough that we had one of the quad chairs to ourselves. I figured that by eleven or so it would pick up. A lot of tourists didn't get up in time for the early runs.

We decided to do one easy run to warm up, and then we would work the Nastar course. It was a timed slalom course that was open to the public. There was a fee to use it, of course, but I liked the chance to push for my best times. After buckling my skis, I pushed off, loving the way they cut through the soft powder, tips playing peek-a-boo as they sliced through the various depths. Powder was fun, and I liked to go slow and play. LeMoyne caught up with me quickly and went off to the right.

Together we did big S-cuts down the hill, perfectly synchronized. We got faster as we went, cutting the turns a little sharper, a little closer together each turn, until we were no longer turning, just in a full-out race, sitting back on our skis and appearing to float down the mountain.

I let up as we reached the flats in front of the lift and let LeMoyne win.

We got back on the lift, both a little winded.

LeMoyne let out a coyote howl. "That was fun, man."

"Powder. We don't get nearly enough." We frequently got a dusting or even a couple of inches, but it took at least six inches to get the feel of powder skiing.

"Woo-hoo-hoo!" LeMoyne hollered.

I glanced down. Two skiers were cutting tracks through the Nastar course.

I grinned. "So what are we racing for?"

"You're kidding, right? I ain't racin' you."

"No fun if you ain't racin'," I said.

"No way, man."

"I'll spot you three seconds."

LeMoyne tilted his head to one side. "We're racin' for a six-pack. And you're giving me five seconds."

"Five? No way! That's robbery!"

"Then we ain't racin'."

"Fine by me."

We rode the rest of the way in silence. As we skied up to the starting gates, I said, "Four seconds for a six-pack."

"Okay."

We slid up, our boots centered over the line that had been painted in the snow. We couldn't see each other, but we didn't need to. I watched the four starting lights go out, one at a time, and I started counting.

"One-Mississippi . . ."

Now I could see LeMoyne in front of me, cutting the turns around the poles, but not nearly close enough. He barely brushed them.

"Two-Mississippi . . ."

It was hard watching LeMoyne put so much real estate between us. The girl operating the run stuck her head out of the shack.

"You all right?"

I nodded. "Three . . ."

"You sure?"

In response, I jumped out of the gate. Powder is fun, but it's slow to ski on, especially at the start. I leaned forward, knees bent, totally determined and completely relaxed. As I entered the gates, the only thing on my mind was the hill in front of me.

I twisted in and out of the poles, feeling each one *thunk* my shin pads as I cut my skis right next to it, forcing it to bend down and away from me as I went. Shifting my weight from foot to foot, leaning into a rhythm that was almost perfect, I felt the wind whip past my cheeks. The truly perfect rhythm was the one I found between the moguls, but this was close.

My skis had picked up enough speed to start rattling on the snow.

I was almost three-fourths of the way through the poles when I saw LeMoyne in front of me. I hunched down tighter. Robert would buy the six-pack for either of us, but we would have to pay. And I was not wasting money on a six-pack.

Only now was I starting to feel a slow burn in my thighs. I had to tuck my arms in quickly to avoid getting wrapped up in the gates and then fling them back out for balance as I shifted sideways again. It was a precarious, aggressive balancing act. Catch an edge or catch a pole, and you could be spread out all over the mountainside.

We went into the last six gates together, and I just barely edged him out at the end.

"Oh, you suck!" LeMoyne bellowed.

"But not as much as you do!"

We slid to a stop, spraying snow in front of us like a curtain. I planted my poles in front of me and leaned forward, resting my weight on them. LeMoyne did the same. He was panting heavily.

"You all right?"

He waved a gloved hand at me. "Forgot . . . inhaler . . . today."

"You all right?" I repeated, this time with a degree of alarm.

Nodding, he panted, "Be . . . fine. . . . Just . . . give me . . . a minute."

Catcalls came from the chair passing over us, and I looked up to see a group of four girls waving at us. Then two of them smacked their skis together, sending snow falling and making them laugh even harder. Fortunately, their sense of timing was poor, and the snow fell well short of LeMoyne and me.

"Damn tourists," he said, echoing a popular line.

"Ready to go?"

"Yeah. I probably should go take a hit from my inhaler." His breathing had slowed down, and he wasn't wheezing, but he was still breathing harder than I was.

"All the way home?"

"I keep an extra one at the shop."

We were midway down the mountain. There was a two-person chair one run over—an old, short lift that went back up to the top.

Following my gaze, LeMoyne said, "How 'bout you meet me at the bottom?"

"No, man, it's cool. I'll ski down with you."

"I don't need a babysitter. I'm gonna take it easy all the way down, and it'd drive you nuts. Go tackle a bowl, and I'll meet you at the bottom. Then we'll have a rematch."

"You think you can beat me if you can breathe?"

He grinned. "Absolutely."

"Not a chance." I glanced over to the other lift. "You sure you'll be okay?"

"I'm sure," LeMoyne said. "Meet at the Super Six?"

The Super Six was one of the new six-person chairs, which were supposed to be even faster than the super quads. "Yeah."

"In twenty?"

"You got it," I said, skiing off to the side. "See you in twenty."

- - -

Although I was taking the slow, old chair up to the top and then having to ski twice the distance LeMoyne was going, I wasn't worried about meeting him on time. He would ski easy. And I skied faster than he did even when he was feeling great.

I wished I could help LeMoyne. Even allowing for the effects of the powder, his time on the slalom was slow, and I didn't think he'd make the team. I didn't know how to help him, though. Skiing just came naturally to me, like breathing. Which was something else he couldn't do. I laughed to myself and looked around some more.

The old chair was usually quiet even on busy days; on slow days, it was almost as dead as the rental shop. There were between five and fifteen empty chairs between each rider. I had a chair to myself, and there was a snowboarder about eight chairs in front of me, leaning sideways with one leg up on the bench.

Seemed like people either skied or they snowboarded, and each group hated the other sport. I only knew a handful of people who actually did both. I had tried boarding a few times, and I could take it or leave it. Skiing, though, was essential for my survival.

"Dude!"

I turned around. About four chairs back was another snowboarder. I looked forward again. The snowboarder in front of me was oblivious.

"DUDE!"

He still didn't turn around, so I tried to help out. "Hey, man," I called. "Back here!"

"DUDE!" The shredder behind me sounded like he was going to hurt himself.

"Hey, man!" I yelled.

I turned back around to the second boarder and shook my head. "No ears, man!"

The shredder smiled and raised his hand in acknowledgment. The rest of the ride was quiet.

One of my favorite things about a lot of fresh powder is

its amazing ability to mute and amplify sounds at the same time. The world was absolutely still, but the whining of the chairlift gears almost filled the air.

I thought the shredder would try to get his buddy's attention at the top. But the guy in front of me was off the chair and down the mountain faster than I thought was possible for a snowboarder, and the guy behind me didn't even yell at him.

I decided to skip the bowl and just take a blue to warm my legs back up. I could do a few jumps and play in the powder while it was still so fresh. LeMoyne and I would come do the bowl together.

Like many blue runs, the top was split down the middle, with one half groomed and the other half allowed to keep the moguls. Of course I ran the moguled side. Powder takes control away from the skier, forcing you to skim the tops. It's almost like flying, but you're holding on to control by your toenails.

Jumps were necessary in the powder, of course. I did an Iron Cross first, and actually pulled a helicopter off two moguls in a row. I lost track of the twisters and eagles I did.

I was panting almost as hard as LeMoyne had been by the time I got to the bottom of the mogul field. It was a lot of work, but, man, it was fun!

Letting my skis follow their own lazy course for a few moments, I bounced up and down, shaking off the stress of the run. Slowly, I began tightening up my turns and crossed from the top run over the lip into the lower half.

There were more moguls on the side, so I was right

next to the trees. I settled into the rhythm of the moguls, sinking into it the same way my skis sank into the soft powder. I wondered if LeMoyne had tried cross-country skiing.

Then, suddenly, the world went dark.

- - -

The first thing I knew was that I was on my back.

"Go get the ski patrol!"

Then I realized that I was in pain.

"Oh, thank God you're breathing."

But it was hard to breathe.

"Don't move," a voice said to me as I tried to do just that. Then the voice yelled, "Go to the next lift if you don't see anyone on the way down! And hurry!"

I was able to briefly open my eyes. I forced them to open again, and I saw the sky above me. It was clear blue, almost too bright to look at. Again, I tried to sit up.

"Don't move!" It was definitely a girl, but I couldn't see her.

I tried to speak and couldn't. I swallowed hard and tried again. "Wha . . . ?"

"That maniac slammed right in—Lie still!"

I was trying to get away from the pain on my face. When I opened my eyes again, I saw green ones just a few inches away. "Ow!"

"I'm trying to stop the bleeding," she said in an apologetic voice.

"With what? An ice pick?"

"A snowball. It's the best I can do right now."

I tried to push her hand away, but either she was Supergirl or I still didn't have full control of my body back. Breathing was easier now, but I felt like Jell-O all over. I must have had the wind knocked out of me.

"What happened?"

I was able to focus on her a little better now. She looked familiar as she shook her head in disgust and said, "Some idiot on a snowboard came flying out of the trees and slammed right into you. He wiped out pretty good, too, but got right up again and took off!" I couldn't stop a whimper and she said, "Sorry," as she quit pushing so hard on my face. "It just pisses me off."

"I can tell."

"Does anything else hurt?" she asked anxiously. "You don't seem to be bleeding from anywhere else that I can see."

"I think I'm okay. What happened?"

She frowned. "I told you, a snow—"

"—boarder came out of the trees and hit me," I finished for her. "You said that. But what really happened? Why are you holding a snowball on my face? How bad am I hurt?" It dawned on me that she was really pale.

"It all happened so fast, I don't really know. The powder just blew up around you, and you were both gone for a few seconds. Then the snow settled, and you lost both poles and a ski, and the jerk just lost his hat—" She broke off. "Are you okay?"

As soon as she said that, I realized my left leg was twisted underneath me. "Yeah. I just need to get up—"

"You can't," she said firmly, putting a hand on my chest. "You have a head injury, probably a neck injury, too, and—"

"What are you, a doctor?"

"I lifeguard in the summers," she said with authority. "I'm trained in first aid."

"But I need to—"

"Stay still," she ordered.

Watching her, I said, "We need a cross."

"Excuse me?"

"Use your poles or skis and make a cross above us, so people know we're here. We don't want to get run over."

"Oh. Right. Hold this." She took my hand and placed it on the snowball that was covering the right side of my face. She picked up her skis and took a few awkward steps up the hill before planting the back of each of them deep in the snow. While her back was turned, I was able to sit up a little and at least get my leg out from under me.

From my new vantage point, I realized something was wrong with the mountain. Suddenly, my stomach heaved. There was blood splattered all over the closest three moguls. Maybe staying still wasn't such a bad idea. Fighting the growing panic, I lay back down and focused on watching her.

"Hard to move around in these boots," she grumbled as she settled back. "I've seen the distress sign before. I just forgot. And I thought it was an X, not a cross." She didn't try to take over holding the snowball on my face. I was a little disappointed.

"Have we met?" I asked her.

Grinning and raising an eyebrow, she replied, "You mean you could forget meeting me?"

"No, I mean, yes, I mean—" I put my other hand up to my head. "Not fair when I have a headache."

She laughed. "You work at the ski shop, right?"

It clicked. "You brought your friend in for poles yesterday."

"Cousin."

"Huh?"

"She's my cousin."

"Oh. I thought you lived down 70."

"I do. But my cousin and her friends are up here for the week, and since I know my way around and have my own car, I got invited to join them. They're up here for an early senior trip."

I choked on a laugh.

"What?" she asked.

"I'll tell you later." Then I asked, "What's your name?"

"Why?"

"I should know the name of my heroine."

"I'm nobody's heroine."

"My Florence Nightingale, then."

She laughed, but it was an irritated, disbelieving laugh. "My name's Angela."

"Hi, Angela. My name's Sandro."

"Hello, Sandro. That's an unusual name."

"I'm an unusual guy."

"I bet. Are you in ROTC?" she asked.

"In what-C?"

"ROTC. You know, the high school military training program or something."

"Do I look like I'd be in that?"

"Well, yeah, with your buzz cut."

"Oh," I said, reaching for my head. "That."

"Yeah. That. It's not the style I see most ski bums wearing."

"I'm not a ski bum."

"Oh. Sorry."

We were quiet for a few moments. I wanted to sit up, but I was afraid Angela might give me a concussion slamming me back down to the ground. I was also starting to get cold. "Who'd you send to get the ski patrol?"

"My cousin and her friends."

"Do they know how to ski or were they going to walk down the slope?"

"They have been gone awhile, haven't they?"

"Mmm-hmm."

"Maybe I should go see if I can find somebody." She didn't sound like she wanted to go.

"Someone will be coming soon," I said. "If there wasn't a patrol close by, it could take a while to get up here. And they won't be coming till your cousin gets there. Can she ski?"

"She's okay. It's her friends who will be slowing her down." Angela shook her head. "I should have gone downhill and had her stay here."

"No thanks!"

"You almost sound glad that I'm here."

"I am," popped out before I could stop it. "Your cousin seemed like a handful," I added.

"Yeah, well, when people charge her for a full day when the last hour's supposed to be free—"

"You knew?" Focusing on the conversation was a little hard, but I was afraid that if I stopped trying, the world would go fuzzy again.

"I can read."

"But she didn't bother to. And you didn't tell her."

"Nope."

"I get the feeling you and your cousin aren't real close."

"Meghan's okay. We used to be good friends. But in the last couple of years"— Angela shrugged—"I'm not as cool as she thinks I should be."

"That's because she's damn cold."

Angela laughed. "She's still using those poles," she pointed out.

"She'll be paying a late fee, then."

"I don't think that will bother her."

"Which is why you didn't mind her paying full price."

"Something like that."

We sat in an agreeable silence for a few moments.

"Hear that?" I asked.

"What?" We were quiet again, and then she smiled. "Snowmobile?"

"Ski patrol," I said. "Can I sit up now?"

"No." She gave me a glare. "You can't make me look bad just as they're getting here!"

"Ah. I see."

"What?"

"You just want to show off your first-aid skills to the ski patrol. You're looking to change careers." The snowmobile had reached us.

"Shut up," she said. I started laughing.

"You can't be hurt too bad if you're laughing like that," the patroller said as he walked over. "What happened?"

"Collision," Angela said.

"You've got blood all over," he said to her. "Where are you hurt?"

Startled, I turned my head to see where she was bleeding.

"I'm fine," she said. "He's got the bad cut."

Now I could see why the patrolman was confused. "How'd I get blood all over your coat?" She looked like she had been in a fight. I'd have to pay to get it cleaned, but I wasn't sure if the blood would even come out.

"Probably when I first got to you and had to roll you over."

"He lost consciousness?" the patroller asked. He hadn't taken his eyes off her.

"Yes."

"For how long?"

Angela thought for a moment. "Not too long. Maybe a minute."

"Can I get up now?" I asked.

"Sandro! Man, didn't realize it was you."

"You weren't looking," I said dryly. Fritz had more girlfriends than anyone I knew. "Can I sit up?"

"Sure, if you think you can."

"Don't you need to check him first or something?" Angela asked.

"How long have you been waiting here?"

"Five or ten minutes."

"Sandro, can you feel all your fingers and toes? Can you move them?"

"Yeah."

"Go ahead and sit up."

As I sat up slowly, still holding the snowball to my face, Angela crossed her arms over her chest. "You're not being very cautious, considering there's been a head injury."

"He's got a really thick skull," Fritz said. He could tell she wasn't impressed. "He's conscious, talking well, recognizes people, and wants to get up. He'll be fine." Just then, I removed the snowball from my face. "Whoa! Sandro!"

Fritz whipped some gauze out of his kit and practically slapped it on my face. "You get a free ride down."

"I'm not riding a sled down the mountain," I said, throwing the bloodied snowball into the trees.

"Yes, you are. That's going to take stitches. And she's right," he added. "We need to do a thorough check for head injury."

"I'm not riding a sled down the mountain."

"You lost consciousness. You can't mess with that."

"I'm a skier, not a sledder," I grumbled.

"You're being stupid," Angela announced.

"I didn't ask you."

"Oh, that's nice. Yeah, I just sat here and took care of you in the cold while my friends went skiing off."

"I didn't ask you to."

"No," she said. "You didn't." She looked at Fritz. "Where are you going to take him?"

"The first-aid station at the bottom of Aurora's Shine Run."

"Okay. I'll drop his skis off there."

"You're not touching my skis!" I growled.

She ignored me and began climbing uphill to get her skis out of the snow.

"Angela!"

Fritz pushed harder on my face. "Hold this. I need to get another one and some tape."

"Angela!" She had pulled her skis out, and simply sat down and let herself slide down to her poles and my ski. Then she began cleaning the snow from the bottom of her boots.

She was stepping into her first ski when I said, "I'm sorry, Angela. I didn't mean it."

Her second binding locked her boot in. Fritz was taping my face, and I couldn't see her.

"Angela, please."

Finally, Fritz leaned back. Angela was holding her poles and my ski.

Fritz reached out. "Here. We usually just strap the skis and poles next to our victim . . . er, passenger."

Angela shook her head. "You'll let him ski down."

"No, I won't." She gave him a doubtful look. "I'd lose my job. Seriously. After a head injury, I have to bring him down in the sled."

She handed him my ski, and I started to let out a sigh of relief. Then she said, "You take this. I'll take the other ones."

"Damn it!" I swore.

Fritz grinned, but he didn't look away from Angela. "Will you wait there?"

"No," she said, and then she finally did look at me again. "There's nothing to wait for." And with that she slid downhill to gather my other pole and ski and then left.

Fritz and I watched her for a minute. Then he said, "Looks like you lost your date."

"She wasn't my date."

"Come on," Fritz said, leaning down and grabbing my hand. "Let's get you loaded on the sled."

"This sucks," I said as he pulled me up.

"You'll be all right."

"I've always been able to ski off the mountain."

"You ever ride a snowmobile?"

"Nope."

"Just think of it as your first ride, then."

"You gonna let me ride behind you?"

"Sure," he said with a grin. "All the way behind me on the sled."

After eight stitches and a call to Mom, I was released from the first-aid station, with strict instructions to go straight home. Angela was as good as her word. My ski and pole were waiting at the first-aid station for me.

She, however, wasn't.

When I walked into the shop the next morning, Robert, LeMoyne, and Kolton were all setting up for the day. LeMoyne was the first to see me.

"You punked out on me! You totally punked!"

"I was—"

"No, no, no, man," LeMoyne said, holding up both hands. "No excuses. You punked. You were chicken 'cause you knew I was gonna beat you!"

"Only place you'll ever beat me is in your dreams!" I retorted as I walked around the counter to go hang my coat in the back room.

"Why'd you—Holy crap!" He broke off as I turned toward him. "What's wrong with your face?"

"I was tryin' to tell you, man, but you didn't want to listen."

"Looks nasty," Robert said, coming to inspect me. "Hey, Kolton, you need to see this."

The slice started just below my right eye and extended

midway down my cheek. It was only deep at the top, though, and that's where the stitches were.

It was kind of scary when I first realized how close I had come to losing my eye. Last night, it hadn't looked that bad, but this morning, nearly the whole right side of my face was swollen and a strange shade of purple. They had warned me about that at the first-aid station, because of the snowball causing mild frostbite, but it still looked freaky.

I stood behind the front counter, coat in hand, waiting to be inspected.

Kolton came over from the boots and whistled low. "You should practice a few times without a blade before you try shaving for real."

LeMoyne grinned, but Robert was shaking his head. "It doesn't look funny to me, Kolton."

"Doesn't feel funny, either," I muttered.

"What'd you do?" Kolton asked.

"I didn't do anything. I just went skiing."

"You hit a tree?"

"I'm not a tree-hugger, and you know it," I said. "Some stupid shredder lost control and took it out on me."

"How bad does he look?" LeMoyne wanted to know.

"Don't know. He took off."

"Seriously?" Robert asked.

"Didja get a fix on him?" LeMoyne asked.

"Ski patrol catch up with him?" Kolton asked.

"Don't think so. I never even saw him. One second, I'm skiing, next second, the world's dark."

"He knocked you out?" Kolton frowned. "You okay to work today?"

"Yeah, I'll be fine."

Kolton gave me an appraising look. "You may feel okay, but you look downright scary."

"You can't send me home," I said, almost panicking. "You know I need the hours."

"Nah, I wouldn't do that. But I *will* send you to the back room so you don't frighten anybody. You can do repairs today. It's about time Robert worked on his customer-service skills anyway."

"Are you trying new material for a comedy club or something? 'Cause you're just a regular joker this morning," Robert grumbled.

Kolton waved Robert away. "Go get the rest of the boots set up," he said. Then he glanced at the clock. "And hurry up. We open in five minutes."

"Who else is workin' today?" I asked.

"Jade and Elizabeth are on the schedule," LeMoyne said.

"Here comes Elizabeth," I said as she pulled open the door.

I picked up my coat to go into the back room.

Kolton said, "LeMoyne, call Jade and tell her to get her butt over here."

Kolton followed me back into the office. "Thought you were going to fire her if she was late again," I said.

"I'd like to, believe me."

"But?"

"But I don't have any applications in right now. And I

need all the help I have for the holiday rush. You know that."

He began rifling through some papers on his desk. Elizabeth came in to hang up her coat and made a fuss over me, but she was pretty cool about it. I went through the office to the repair room and turned my attention to the skis and their paperwork. I was working on my first pair when Kolton got up to unlock the front doors.

I got into fixing the skis, and time flew by. Jade stuck her head in the back room to say she'd buy me dinner after work, since I had covered her shift the day before.

From the office I heard, "Hey, Kolton, you got a second?"

"What's up, LeMoyne?"

"Could you come out here?" I glanced up and caught LeMoyne giving me an odd look.

"What's—"

"Please?"

Looking worried, Kolton got up quickly and went out to the floor with LeMoyne. They disappeared around the corner. I was tempted to go see what was happening. But Kolton would get pissed if we were all gawking or gossiping while there were customers around. LeMoyne would catch me up when it got slow.

Kolton cleared his throat, and I looked up in surprise to see him standing awkwardly in the doorway.

"What's up?"

With a strange look on his face, Kolton said, "I think maybe you should come out here for a second."

"Okay," I said, setting the screwdriver down and wiping my hands on my pants as I came toward him. He didn't move out of the doorway and I stopped a few feet away from him. "Is everything all right?"

"It may be nothing," he said slowly, "but there's a guy here. . . ."

I waited, but Kolton didn't seem to know how to finish whatever it was he was going to say. "There's a guy here? Does he have a gun? Or a million dollars?"

"He has a name."

"A name?" I repeated blankly.

Kolton lifted a rental sheet and looked down at it. "Alessandro Scarpettarini." He looked back up at me. "He . . . he looks a lot like you," he said slowly.

I stared at Kolton, but I wasn't seeing him. I was remembering all the times Mom had told me the story of her hero, Alessandro Something from Italy. A skier who would be back. That was, after all, why we lived here. We were waiting for him to come back. But her whole story had so many holes, it couldn't all be true. And even if it was, there was no way Alessandro Something would be renting skis. As a ski pro, he'd have his own equipment.

"Sandro?"

I blinked and came back to earth. "Yeah. Okay." I grinned, making my cheek hurt, and somehow that was good. "Might as well take a peek."

Kolton still didn't move. He was measuring me with his eyes, looking for something, but I wasn't sure what. And I didn't want to ask. "You sure?" he said.

"Yeah. I mean, I know it's not him. But I've never met another Alessandro. That's gotta be worth something." I cleared my throat. "What'd you say his last name is?"

Kolton had to look at the paper again. "Scarpettarini."
I nodded. "Okay."

I followed Kolton out to the floor. It was the end of morning rush, so the shop wasn't packed. Even if it had been, though, I wouldn't have had to ask Kolton where the other Alessandro was.

He was waiting at the counter, leaning against it in the same place I had been when Angela and her cousin had come in.

He could have been my twin. His black hair was longer, flaunting the natural curls my mother loved to talk about. It had more than just a dash of salt running through it, though. And he had a few wrinkles, but not many, considering he had to be at least twenty years older than me. Even the way he was resting against the counter and toying with the pen looked too much like me.

I wanted to run out, or maybe just vanish back into the repair room until he was gone. He was talking to Robert about something and hadn't seen me. He'd never know.

The bells above the door rang, and I thought it was strange that I could hear them through the bizarre ringing my ears seemed to be doing on their own. Then I saw my mother standing behind him.

I began to move forward quickly, hoping to get to her before she said anything, hoping to get her away from him before he could turn around and see her.

She was scanning the shop, starting with the far side. As she turned her head, she saw me coming toward her.

"Alessandro," she began. She was excited about something. The man in front of the counter turned around.

"Sandro, guess who I talked to last—" She broke off abruptly, focusing on his face.

"Tiffany?" the man said with an odd mixture of hope and disbelief.

"Alessandro?" Mom breathed, with more emotion for my name than I had ever heard.

"Tiffany," he repeated, almost sighing.

Her eyes filled with tears, and, for a long, impossible moment they simply stared at each other. Then she practically threw herself into his arms.

For the first time in years, she had come looking for me. Until this moment, I hadn't been sure she even knew where I worked. She had come looking for *me*. But she found him instead.

- - -

It seemed like everything should have stopped, or maybe the whole world should have just blown up right then, but it didn't. I heard Elizabeth and Jade talking to a couple of customers, and I heard the bells above the door ringing as someone else came in. I felt Kolton's hand come down on my shoulder as I started to shake, and I saw LeMoyne watching me even as he handed a pair of poles to a college kid. Mom, Alessandro, and I seemed to be the only ones stuck in the time warp.

It felt like all the air had been sucked out of the shop. I couldn't breathe. I bolted for the door, running past my mom.

She didn't even notice.

I threw the door open hard enough that it hit the wall and the top window pane cracked. At least I could breathe again. I started walking fast. People moved out of my way.

I got all the way to the corner of Main Street before I realized I was freezing. I had left my jacket in the repair room. Swearing, I turned around. I didn't want to go back and get it, but I wasn't completely stupid. I couldn't walk all the way home without a coat.

"Here," Kolton said, handing me my jacket.

"Thanks," I said, blinking. I hadn't even seen him standing right in front of me.

"You okay?" he asked as I pulled my coat on.

"Sure," I said brightly. "Why wouldn't I be?"

Kolton didn't answer, just watched me with those measuring eyes.

"Mind if I take today off?" I asked. "I've kind of got a headache, and you were just going to stick me in the repair room anyway. And since Jade actually showed up today—"

"Sure," Kolton said. "No problem."

"Thanks, man." I couldn't take my eyes off the shop doors. "She still in there?"

"Yeah."

"I gotta get out of here."

"Want to go hang out at my place?" He stuck his hand in his pocket, fishing for his keys.

"Where's Torey?"

"Ah, man, she's at home. I'm sorry, I just—"

"It's okay."

"You could go hang out with her. She thinks you're cool."

"No man, thanks anyway," I said.

"Sandro?"

We both turned. Angela was walking out of the parking lot, carrying a couple of poles.

"Hey, Angela," I said. "I'm sorry about yesterday. I mean, thanks for yesterday." I wasn't making any sense, so I just shut up.

She tilted her head to look at me. "It almost looks worse today."

"I know. But at least you're looking better."

Kolton gave me a grin. "I'd better get back to the shop."

"That's where I was going," Angela said. "To return these." She held up the poles her cousin had rented.

"Here," Kolton said quickly, "I'll take them for you."

"Okay," Angela said doubtfully. "But I think I owe you some money for them. My cousin kind of kept them longer than she said she would."

"We'll cover it," Kolton said, giving her a wink. "Just do me a favor and take care of him today."

She sniffed. "He prefers to take care of himself."

"Usually," Kolton agreed. "But today he needs a friend." He nodded at me. "Don't be stupid. Play nice. And I'll see you tomorrow."

"Thanks, Kolton," I said as he walked away.

Angela and I looked at each other for a few seconds. She looked away first, blushing a little.

"I like your jacket," I said. I think originally it was a hot pink with some black trim, but it was pretty worn.

"At least it's clean."

"You left before I could offer to pay to get your other one cleaned."

"All you were offering yesterday was attitude."

Deciding that was a dangerous topic, I asked, "You're not skiing today?"

"Meghan and her friends flew out this morning."

"And she asked you to return the poles?"

"No. She wasn't going to."

"I knew she was cold," I said.

"My uncle's got a lot of money. She could afford another pair of poles."

Against my will, I looked down the street to the rental shop. The door was still shut, but I didn't know how soon my mom and this Alessandro Scarpettarini would be walking out of it. I was terrified of them seeing me. So I did something I had never done before.

"You want to go get lunch?"

And just like that, I had a date.

5

I was almost surprised when Angela said "yes," and I honestly didn't know if it was a good sign or bad.

It sure started off bad. I took her to the lodge at the base of Mount Aurora. The restaurants in town would get uptight if you just hung out for a few hours, ordering nothing but sodas or tea and eating their crackers. But at the lodge, you could hang out as long as you wanted to, eating as much or as little as you wanted.

If Angela thought it was strange, she didn't say anything. And that was the problem. She wasn't saying anything— at all.

We got our food and found a table in a back corner. It was empty because it didn't have a view of the mountain, but I didn't care. Watching skiing was not something I wanted to do right now.

After we had sat in silence for so long that I was sure she was going to get up and leave, she smiled. A bright, warm smile just for me.

"What?" I asked.

"You look like the world has ended, and, damn it, I'm going out with a smile on my face!"

For a second I just stared at her. "You're odd."

"This from a guy who invited me to lunch and then didn't say another word for"—she consulted her watch—"almost a whole fifteen minutes."

"I've said a few things."

She raised her eyebrows.

"I asked you if you wanted a hamburger or bratwurst," I muttered, picking up a french fry.

"And you asked if I wanted a Coke or 7-Up."

"See? I've been nothing but courteous."

"You haven't been courteous since I met you," she said flatly.

"Then why are you here with me?"

"I don't know," she said, looking confused. "Honestly, I don't even know why I drove all the way up here just to return those stupid poles."

"I'm glad you did," I said quietly.

She laughed. "You said you were glad I stayed with you on the mountain yesterday right before you got really rude."

"I'm sorry. I came across as a jerk—"

"You *were* a jerk."

"—and I didn't mean to. I was just mad about the situation."

"You didn't have to take it out on me," she pointed out.

"I know, and I'm sorry. How many times are you going to make me say it?"

"How many times will you?"

"One more."

She grinned and lifted her chin.

"I'm truly sorry," I said as sincerely as I could.

"Okay," she said softly. "Now tell me what's wrong today."

"You'll think I'm nothing but trouble."

"I already know that."

I picked up another french fry and then tossed it back in the basket. What little appetite I had was gone. "Are you done?" I asked. She nodded, and I gathered our trash and threw it away.

"What's your life like?" I asked as I pulled the chair out a little bit more from the table before sitting down.

"What do you mean?"

"Well, you live in Golden, right?"

"Yeah."

"With your parents?"

"Yeah."

"You've got your own car and probably a cell phone, too."

"Are you going to tell me about my life and then make me guess about yours?" she asked crossly.

"Okay, okay, so tell me about your life."

She sighed. "My mom, dad, sister, and I live in a house in a pretty nice development. I'm a junior, and I'm on the swim team and soccer team. I like movies and poetry. In the summer, I'm a lifeguard, and I go rafting when I can. And now I feel like I'm a contestant on *Elimidate* or *The Dating Game* or something."

I had been staring out at the rest of the lodge. When she

said she felt like a contestant, I looked at her and grinned. "If you're a contestant, I'm glad I'm the only other player."

She blushed, a bright shade of red, and, for some reason, that made me feel better. She looked down at the table and said, "So tell me about your life."

Whenever someone used to ask me that, I'd launch into my mother's sappy story, loving the way I had mastered the narrative and delivered it like a professional actor. Not today. I looked away from her quickly and scanned the lodge again.

"Or at least tell me what's wrong," she said quietly. "Your friend seemed pretty worried."

"That's my boss." She just looked at me for a second, and I added, "And he's my friend, too."

Angela picked up her Coke and took a drink. Then she just turned the cup in slow circles on the table in front of her and waited.

I took a deep breath and forced my voice to stay calm, "I saw my father today."

"How often do you see him?"

"Maybe I didn't say that right. I saw my father for the *first time* today," and as Angela's eyes got big, I added, "I think."

"You met your father for the first time, and you're sitting here talking to me?"

"No."

"Sandro, are you just giving me a load of crap?"

"No. I haven't ever *met* my father. But I'm pretty sure I *saw* him about a half hour ago."

"But you're not sure?"

When I shook my head, she covered her face with both hands. She took a deep breath and then held her hands at her temples. "You're just messing with me, aren't you? You think I'm an easy target and you—"

"No, Angela, seriously. Nothing like that. Seriously."

"You've never met your father?"

"Never wanted to."

"But you think you saw him today?"

"Yeah. It wrecked my day. Until I saw you," I added hurriedly.

"I don't know if I want to hear this story or not."

"It's a long one," I said. "But I can give you just the CliffsNotes version."

She grinned and leaned forward on her elbows. "You've got thirty seconds."

"It'll take at least sixty."

Angela considered for a second. "Yeah, I can spare a minute."

"When my mom was seventeen, she came up here for spring break. On the second day, she met a guy, and ditched her friends to shack up with him for the rest of the week. When she got home, she tried to reach him, but he gave her all phony stats. Then she found out that I was going to be coming along soon. Her dad kicked her out. She came here to wait for him. And she's been waiting for over seventeen years now." I took a breath. "She's been waiting for him, like she thought they really had something. Which is total-ly stupid, because he totally used her and bailed. And now the bastard's actually come back. Check that. *I'm* the bastard. I don't know what *he* is." I glanced at her. "How am I doin' on time?"

Angela made a little squeak, but didn't say anything. So I kept going.

"So he shows up at the rental shop. Did I mention that he actually told Mom he was an Olympic skier? And she believed him? So what the hell is he doing at a rental shop, if he's such a skier? Messing up my life again," I answered for myself.

"If you've never met him, how did you know it was him?"

"Kolton—my boss—saw his name on the rental agreement. And he looks a lot like me. Or, I guess, I look almost exactly like him."

"You can look like a lot of people," she said. "But it doesn't make you related to them."

"I know. But there aren't many Alessandros that come through town."

"So? You think you and he are the only Alessandros in the world?"

I rolled my eyes and continued, "But that's not the best part. No, the best part is that my mother, who hardly ever even talks to me, came to the shop for the first time ever this morning. So guess who she got to see?"

"Your father." Angela's eyes were huge.

"Oh, yeah. She saw him, and that was it."

"What was it like?" she asked, leaning forward again. "What did they say to each other?"

"Nothin'."

"*Nothing?* After seventeen years?"

"Well, she said his name—"

"She recognized him first?"

"No, she was talking to me." I was trying to tell the whole story, but she kept interrupting.

"Oh."

"So he turns around, and he says her name—"

"So *he* recognized *her.*"

"Yeah. And then they just—"

"What?"

"They just, like, slammed together in a hug."

"How romantic!" she sighed.

"What?"

"Well, think about it—"

"I am," I said dryly.

"After seventeen years, to find the love of your life—"

"He's not the love of her life," I said flatly.

"How can you say that? She's been waiting for him, hasn't she?"

"She's an idiot who got knocked up."

"This is your mother you're talking about!"

"Yeah."

"That's how you feel about your mother?" Angela said in disbelief.

"Yeah. She blew a full-ride scholarship. She lost her family. She's stayed in this stupid town, barely making ends meet, because she *actually thought* he was going to come back for her."

"And he just did."

"Seventeen years later," I said. "He's not here looking

for her. He's here for vacation. But she's so stupid, she's gonna think he's here for her."

"You really think your mother's stupid?"

"I know she is."

"Wow." Angela dropped back in her chair. "Wow."

"What?"

"You have some serious issues."

"Excuse me?"

"I can't believe the contempt you have for your own mother."

"If you met her, you'd understand."

"But from what you've said . . . " She shook her head and then continued, "She got pregnant and was kicked out of her house."

"Yeah."

"She then proceeded to raise you and take care of you, all by herself, without a college education."

"In a manner of speaking."

"What do you mean by that?"

"She's raised me, but that's about it. She's spent my whole life just waiting for him."

"And there's something wrong with that?"

I stared at her. "You're kidding, right?"

Angela shrugged. "Have you looked at it from her point of view?"

"She's too confused to have a point of view."

"She gave up everything to keep you."

"Wrong. She gave up everything and kept me so she'd have leverage when Alessandro returned."

"Wow."

"Would you quit saying that?"

"I'm sorry. It just seems like the only thing I can say. You have no respect for your mother. And it doesn't seem like you have respect for anybody else, either," she added.

"Respect has to be earned."

"It has to be given a chance before it can be earned."

I shook my head. "You don't get it. You've got your nice TV-sitcom family at home, and you just don't get it."

"Oh, I get it," she retorted. "You don't."

"What don't I get?"

"That your mother did the best she could. That you've got a good life here, with more opportunities than most. That *no one* has a perfect life."

I was staring at her. "Are you always so—" I had to search for the word "—prissy?"

"Prissy?" she repeated in disbelief. "Me?"

Too late, I knew I had made a mistake. I wished I could take it back. I wished I could take it all back, start the whole lunch over again.

She stood up. "Thank you for lunch," she said. "I'm going home now."

"Angela, I'm sorry," I said as she walked away.

She didn't look back as she went through the lodge and out the doors. If I could have left that way, I would have, too.

But what I really wanted to do was think of something to say to her, something that would make up for the jerk I had been, something that would get her to come back and sit with me. Instead, I got up and went back to the snack bar for another 7-Up.

- - -

Ringing the doorbell was hard. When Torey answered, in a T-shirt, sweats, and mussed-up hair, I wished the ground would just swallow me up.

"Oh my God, Sandro!" she exclaimed. "Are you okay?"

"Yeah," I said, wondering why she was flipping out. I didn't usually just show up at people's houses, but it wasn't that late. Just a little after six.

"What happened?"

I stared at her blankly, then remembered my face. "Oh, I had an accident yesterday."

"It looks just awful. What am I doing? Come on in." She opened the door wide.

"No, thanks, I didn't mean to interrupt—"

She laughed and grabbed my arm, pulling me in. "Don't be stupid. It was my day off, and I've just been lounging around. Kolton ran out to get a pizza. He'll be back in a second. Have a seat," she finished, almost shoving me into a beat-up old rocker. "Tell me what happened."

As quickly as I could, I gave her the story of the hit-and-run shredder.

"What an ass," was her assessment. "Can I get you something to drink?" she asked as she disappeared into the kitchen.

"No, thanks," I said, shifting uncomfortably. "Kolton still doesn't trust Pizza Pie, huh?"

She set some plates and napkins back on the end table and then dropped onto the couch. "He never will again."

"What did they do that was so wrong?"

"Sardines instead of pepperoni, in a stuffed pie."

"Ugh," I said, making a face. "So he didn't even know that the sardines were in there until—"

"He bit into it," she said with me. "So now he goes to place the order and then stays there to make sure they get it right."

"'Za's here!" Kolton called as he came in the door.

"We're right here, honey. You don't have to yell," Torey scolded.

"That wasn't yellin'," he said with a grin. "Hey, Sandro, good to see you."

"How were things at the shop today?"

"They were all right. Jade was mad I made her stay for the afternoon, but I think it will be good for her in the long run."

"Build some character?" I asked.

"Somethin' like that," he agreed.

"I didn't know you ever had weekends off, Sandro," Torey said as she handed Kolton a plate. "I thought you always worked weekends and that's why you don't ski on the team."

"Hey," Kolton said, "you're supposed to be nice to our guest."

"It's all right," I said. Then I told Torey, "I wasn't feeling great this morning, and Kolton let me take the day off." Kolton glanced at me but didn't say anything.

She leaned over and gave him a kiss. "That's my guy," she said.

Kolton put a piece of pizza on a plate and then tried to hand it to me. When I shook my head, he growled, "Take it.

You don't come to my house and then just sit and watch us eat."

"Thanks," I said, taking the plate from him.

We ate dinner and watched a couple of sitcom reruns. Kolton actually offered me a beer, which drew an angry look from Torey, but I didn't feel like drinking.

"So," I said, finally deciding it was pointless to try to keep Torey out of the loop, "did my mom say anything interesting before she left the shop?"

Kolton shook his head and took a swig of beer. "They were still just standing there when I went back in. Then they left together. I don't think either of them said a word the entire time. She had a pretty good grip on his arm as they went out the door, though. Like she thought he was going to disappear right in front of her."

"Oh, he'll disappear all right, but give it a week or so."

"Who's this?" Torey asked.

"My father."

"Ooohhh," she said, eyebrows disappearing under her bangs.

"He left without renting anything," Kolton said, reaching into his back pocket. "But he did leave this." He handed me the rental agreement.

"Thanks," I said. I didn't unfold it. I didn't really need to. I knew the form very well, and knew that Kolton had just handed me not only my father's first and last name, but his address, phone number, age, height, and weight as well. It was strange to think that after so many years I had all that information right in my hands.

"So who was that this morning?" he asked.

"My rescuer."

"What?"

"She was there when I got plowed over yesterday, and she stuck a snowball on my face to stop the bleeding. Her name's Angela."

"She's cute," he said, suffering Torey's light punch on the shoulder.

"She hates me."

Kolton laughed. "She can't hate you too much. She was looking for you this morning."

"Maybe," I said. "But she hates me now."

"Why?" Torey asked.

I looked at my hands. "Because now she knows me."

"In one day?" Torey said doubtfully.

"It was bizarre. I told her everything. It was like I couldn't shut up. And now she hates me."

"See, man, if you had just listened to me, this wouldn't be a problem," Kolton said, shaking his head.

"What?"

"How many times have I told you that you need to talk to someone . . . that you need to see a shrink?"

"And me spending time on a black couch would have solved this?"

"You used her as your shrink," he said.

"I what?"

"You told her everything because she was a stranger. Sometimes it's easier to talk to a stranger," Torey said.

"Exactly," Kolton agreed. "But if you had been going to see a shrink, you wouldn't have needed to talk to a stranger. You could have played it cool."

I leaned my head back. "Too late to play it cool now," I said miserably. "She hates me. And I don't blame her."

"Call her," Torey said. "Right now. Call her and apologize."

"Yeah," Kolton agreed. "She'll forgive you. She digs you, man."

"I can't call her," I said. "I don't have her number. Hell, I don't even know her last name."

6

Our refrigerator was well-stocked, for us. But it still didn't have any milk or juice. Sighing, I grabbed the last yogurt and let the door swing shut. I jumped. Then I swore. "You've got to be kidding me!"

Alessandro was standing on the other side of the refrigerator, wearing boxers and a T-shirt.

"I don't believe this!"

He was just standing there, staring at me.

"Did I grow a third eye?" I demanded.

"I told you he was as handsome as you," my mother said, coming into the kitchen.

"Hard to tell with his face all purple," he replied.

Mom swatted him lightly. "Be nice," she scolded, not meaning anything.

"What the hell are you doing up?" I asked. I couldn't remember the last time I had seen her out of bed before eleven. Between working nights and not being a morning person, she always said it wasn't worth pretending to be awake.

"Alessandro and I are catching up on things," she said, wrapping her arms around his midsection and kissing the back of his neck.

Shaking my head, I left the yogurt on the counter. Instead of feeling hungry, I now felt like I was going to throw up.

"Where are you going?" Mom asked.

"School," I replied, rolling my eyes.

"Not today, Sandro," Mom said.

"Sandrino," he said.

"What?" Mom and I asked together.

"We were all called 'Sandrino' as children—my father, his father, and me." Alessandro nodded toward me. "You are the fourth Alessandro Scarpettarini."

"No," I said shortly, "I'm the first, only, and last Alessandro Birch."

"My son's name is Alessandro Scarpettarini," he declared, Italian dripping off every word.

"Maybe I'll meet him someday."

"Sandro," Mom said, shooting a nervous look at Alessandro as he frowned at me. "Just sit down, okay?"

"Why?"

"Because your father's here! We're going to spend the whole day together, and—" she broke off. "What are you doing?"

"Putting my coat on," I said as I did just that. "I don't want to freeze."

"You're not going to school!"

"I'm not staying here!" I retorted.

"Yes, you are. We've got—"

"I'm leaving," I said.

"Do what your mother tells you!" Alessandro said sharply.

I glared at him. "Shut up."

He stood up and took two quick steps toward me. "I'm your father—"

"You gave me a *cell*! A single cell, and it wasn't even a whole cell—she gave me the other half. You're a donor. That doesn't make you my father."

"Sandro!" Mom gasped.

To my surprise, Alessandro laughed. "You are right. But you don't get that mad unless you really care about something."

"Are you trying to say I care about you?"

"You care about your father. And that is who I am, even if I just 'donated a single cell.'"

I was trembling, and I hated myself for it.

"This is a surprise for both of us. Sit down. Let us talk. I want to know you," Alessandro said.

"I don't want to know you."

Alessandro walked calmly over to the sofa and sat down. Mom practically flew to his side. "You act like I walked out on you and your mother."

"Are you trying to say you didn't?"

"Of course, he didn't!" Mom exclaimed.

"Quit defending him!" I exploded. "Quit acting like he's perfect."

"I don't claim to be perfect—" Alessandro began.

"Good! Just go back to the dukedom or whatever it is and leave us alone!"

He turned to Mom. "What is he talking about?"

Mom was looking at me like I had lost my mind. "I have no idea. Sandro, what *are* you talking about?"

"You said he said he was a duke or something," I muttered.

Mom stared at me and then just started laughing.

"Why did you tell him that?" Alessandro asked her.

"I didn't," Mom said between giggles.

"You did!" I insisted.

"No, Sandro, I never said he was a duke." She looked at him. "*Are* there dukes in Italy?"

My mind was spinning as I went back through everything else that I remembered her telling me as a child. "You said he was a duke and that he was on the Olympic team—"

"Wanted to be," Alessandro interjected.

"What?"

"I wanted to be on the Olympic team, but I wasn't good enough. I barely made the Dartmouth team."

"You got up and left Mom without saying good-bye."

He spread his hands in front of him. "Yes. That I did do."

"You gave her a fake number," I continued triumphantly.

"I did not!"

"And a fake address!" I ignored his interruption. "You never called her, never tried to find her."

"None of this makes any sense! How can you be saying these things?" he asked.

"You're a lying, stealing fraud! And Mom's wasted all

my life just waiting for you!" The world was blurry, and for a second I thought I was going to pass out or something, but then I realized in horror that tears were running down my cheeks.

Angrily, I wiped my sleeve across my face and went to the front door. "I'm outta here."

Neither of them said anything as I pulled the door shut behind me.

I went down the first set of stairs and stopped at the balcony. I rested my arms on the rail, and dropped my head on them. I had a science review for our unit exam today and would probably miss a quiz in calculus, but I really didn't care.

My hand was trembling as I pulled my cigarettes out of my pocket and lit up. I could go to the ski shop. If Kolton didn't need help, I could just hang out. But I didn't feel like walking all the way into town. I didn't even feel like walking to the bus stop. All I wanted to do was curl up in bed and hope Alessandro would just slink back to wherever he had come from.

A door from the flight above me opened and closed, and footsteps started down the stairs. I lifted my head and looked out over the parking lot, hoping that our neighbor would just keep on walking without talking to me.

"You want to tell me what that was all about?" Mom asked. She wasn't shouting, but she wasn't using a comforting tone, either.

"No." I exhaled a plume of smoke.

"Why not?"

"I'm tired of explaining everything to you."

"Well, apparently I need to be explaining things to you more often," she said. "Why on earth did you think he was a duke?"

"Because every time you told me about him, you said he was! He was a duke, he had a place on the Olympic team if he wanted it, then he bailed out on you and wrecked your life! He doesn't deserve another chance!"

"Okay. First off, I never said that. And secondly, he didn't bail out on me."

"He left without saying good-bye! That's bailing!"

"And third . . ." she continued mildly.

"Third what?"

"We were meant to be together. All of us. As a family. You need to give him a chance," she said softly.

"A chance? Why should I?"

"He hasn't done anything wrong, Sandro!"

"He left us—"

"He didn't know I was pregnant! He wasn't leaving *you*." She leaned into me briefly. "If you'll come back inside, we can all talk. We can get this all sorted out."

I looked at her out of the corner of my eyes as I took a long drag. She was wearing an old fleece pullover, her hair was tousled, she didn't have any makeup on, and she looked better than she had in years. She was shining with happiness. "You're going to let him stay, aren't you?"

"We're going to see what we can do," she said simply. But she was smiling so big, you'd think she already had a diamond on her hand.

"Mom, please don't do this. He's just going to use you and leave again," I said.

"He can't do that *again*," Mom said, "because he hasn't done it *before.*"

"Why are you doing this?"

"I love him."

"You don't even know him!"

"We're soul mates," Mom declared. "It's fate."

"Crap," I countered, crushing my cigarette under my foot.

"How can you say that?" she demanded. "How often do I come see you at work? What are the chances that the one time I come in, Alessandro is there, too? It's fate. That's too much for coincidence. It was meant to be."

I looked at her for a long moment, trying to figure out what I wanted to say. "If it really *is* fate, if you're soul mates, it shouldn't be this hard. You shouldn't have to force fate. But that's what you've been trying to do for seventeen years now."

"I've been raising you—"

"No," I said, shaking my head, "I was just the insurance that he'd stick around a little longer the next time."

Mom was quiet for a few seconds. "Is that how you really feel?"

"It's true, isn't it?"

"God, Sandro, how can you even think that?"

"And yet you're still not denying it."

"I wouldn't know where to begin. You're my son, Sandro, and you've been my only family since—"

"The day I was born," I said bitterly.

"Since the day I chose you over them," she said. "I chose you, Sandro. Don't you get it?"

"You were stuck with me." I stood up from the railing. "And now you're going to stick me with him."

"If that's the only way you can see it, then, yes."

Backing away from her slowly, I said, "I'll be back later."

"Where are you going?"

"I don't know," I said.

"When will you come back?"

"I don't know."

- - -

Where I went, of course, was to the slopes. I stopped at the ski shop first, but Kolton didn't have enough customers to let me work for the day, although he did have my paycheck. So I grabbed my skis and headed for the lifts.

I intended to take it easy, since the medic at the first-aid station had advised against strenuous activity until the stitches were out. For me, skiing wasn't strenuous unless I wanted it to be.

The lines were pretty long—even the singles line wasn't moving fast—so I had a lot of time to just stand and watch people. I stretched out while I was waiting, leaning far over my skis both forward and back.

I finally got on the quad with a family. It was a mom, a dad, and a little girl who was about eight. On the mountain, you found two types of tourists: the social ones who wanted to become your best friend in the five-minute ride to the top, and the rude ones who acted almost offended that they had to share the chair with someone not in their group. This family was social. The father in particular had a ton of questions.

Halfway up, they were inviting me to meet them later for lunch. By the time we got to the top, I had such a headache from their incessant talking that I wasn't sure I'd be able to ski, and I sure wasn't going to meet them for lunch.

Of course, I was able to ski, and about midway down, my headache was gone. I decided I'd just stay on the top for a while, and went to catch the old two-person chair. As I skied up to the end of the line, I looked ahead, trying to see if there were any other single skiers. I didn't see any.

"Single?" I called out. It was a good way to move up. And people didn't mind, because in the long run it made things move faster.

"Single?" I yelled again.

"Yo!" More than halfway up the line, I saw a pole waving in the air.

"Excuse me," I said. "Excuse me." And I began moving up the line. It wasn't until I was two people behind the guy holding his pole in the air that I could see who it was. Phil Sirocco.

Sirocco, like half of our school, had a lot of money. He might have been the richest kid there. His parents had moved here when his older brother began the ski competition circuit. I don't know if Sirocco's brother had actually done anything with his skiing, but Phil, according to some, had his sights set on the World Cup next year. During ski season, he was rarely in school more than two days a week.

I had stopped next to an older guy, and he was kind of looking at me. "You gonna go up there?" he asked. I could tell he was ready to suggest I move to the back of the line if I wasn't going to go forward.

Using my poles, I pulled myself up alongside Sirocco.

"Hi th—" he broke off. "Birch."

"Sirocco."

We didn't say anything to each other as we followed the pair in front of us and then got on.

As our chair swung away from the base, he reached up and pulled the leg rest down, still without saying anything.

I reached in my pocket and pulled out a cigarette. I was burning through them today. If I wasn't careful, I'd be over my cigarette budget for the week. As I lit up, Sirocco coughed.

"Must you?" He coughed again. A loud, obnoxious, fake cough.

"Yes," I said, exhaling. "I find it clears the air when things smell bad."

"Then the least you can do is share."

I lifted my eyebrows. "I thought smoking was a no-no for the ski team," I said, holding the pack toward him.

"Leave team rules to team skiers," he advised, using his own lighter. "I didn't know you skied."

As stupid as that comment was, I was surprised when I responded, "Evidently there's a lot you don't know."

We smoked in silence for almost the rest of the ride. As we neared the end of the lift, I grabbed a small chunk of snow from my ski boot and extinguished my cigarette before slipping it back into the pack. Sirocco watched me, then flicked his butt off into the trees.

"You ever do the Nastar course?"

"Yep," I said as I yanked on the leg lift. He made me wait a couple of seconds before he moved his skis off so I could actually raise the bar.

"Hundred bucks says you can't beat me."

"Easy to say when it's daddy's money."

"Oh, that's right. You're one of the charity kids. I'll put my hundred up against whatever you can afford. Ten cents, is it?"

Stung, I retorted, "Fifty and you're on." Fifty was more than I could afford to lose, but if I won—

"Fifty cents? Are you sure?"

"Fifty dollars," I ground out.

"Big spender," he said as we both pushed off the chair and slid off to the right.

"No. I'm not going to lose."

We skied off to the starting gate. The tourists were out in full force today, and they all wanted to show how well they could ski, so we had to wait in another line. Sirocco looked at me. "Can you really cover fifty?"

"Don't have it on me," I admitted. "I won't need it, but I can cover it."

"You're stupid. Don't you know how good I am?"

"Yeah. Almost as good as me."

He laughed. "You got guts. But guts won't get you down the mountain first."

I was relieved when it was finally our turn. I was sick of listening to his trash, and I was ready to ski. We went into the gates, boots up against the wand, leaning forward on our poles, listening to the countdown and watching the starting lights.

The final tone sounded. I grunted and pushed off, leaping up at the same time. Every second would be important. Today the snow was packed and hard—very different conditions from my race with LeMoyne. I had to start my turns earlier, to give my edges a chance. Even so, my old skis had a hard time making the cuts. It was a battle all the way down, my skis wanting to slide out and go away from the gates, my body straining to keep them in the line.

I was tucked as tight as I could be, using my poles to keep my balance as my skis chattered underneath me. My jaw was clenched, both because I was concentrating and because I didn't want to bite my tongue. I never looked for Sirocco; I was totally focused on each gate as it came up. Dimly I was aware of shouts and catcalls coming from people on the lift above us.

As I went around the last gate, I dared to glance to the side. Sirocco was right next to me. I tucked tighter, almost hugging my knees for the small stretch between the last gate and finish line.

Standing up and shifting to one side, I skidded to a stop. So did Sirocco. He looked at me, and I could tell he didn't know who won, either. We both turned to the clocks.

I lost. It was by less than three-tenths of a second, but that didn't change anything. I lost.

For a few seconds we just stood there, panting. My legs felt like hot spaghetti noodles. My thighs especially were burning, almost on fire from all the pressure they had had to put on my skis. I was leaning forward, putting some of my weight on my poles instead. I had a clear view of Sirocco's new, shorter slalom skis. They made mine look almost antique.

When I felt that I could control my voice, I said, "I'll have your money tomorrow. You'll be at school?"

He waved his hand at me. "Don't worry about it. I don't need your money."

No kidding, I thought. But aloud I said, "It was a bet. I pay my debts."

"It was the closest race I've had all season," Sirocco said. "That's enough."

"You'll be at school tomorrow?" I pressed.

"Yeah."

I nodded and pushed off, heading back down the hill. I was having a rotten day, and I figured the best thing to do was go back home. Actually, I was having a rotten few days. Maybe instead of going home, it was time to find a party.

As a rule, parties weren't hard to find during the season. But on a Monday, I'd have to be really lucky to find one. And lately, my luck just wasn't that good.

I took my skis back to the shop. Kolton was busy with a customer, so I just stored my stuff in the back and headed into town.

At the bank, I deposited my paycheck and then had to think for a moment. Finally, I decided on $200 cash for me. Well, $50 for Sirocco, $100 for Mom for rent, and the remaining $50 for me. I'd be stretching it thin till the next paycheck, but I thought I could do it.

When I got my receipt back, I looked with pride at my balance. Nearly three thousand dollars. I'd have no trouble moving, getting my first apartment, and starting my life when I finally graduated from high school. Especially since I was going to move to a town with a reasonable cost of living. I wasn't sure I was ready to leave Colorado, but life was a lot cheaper on the Front Range.

7

"Alessandro? Is that you?"

"Depends which one you mean," I said.

Mom came out of her bedroom. "I'm glad you finally came home."

As I put my jacket on the back of the chair, I said, "He's already gone, huh?"

"He went to get dinner."

"Of course he did. And will he bring it back in another seventeen years, or will it be more like twenty this time?"

"Sandro, if you're going to be rude about this, you can just go someplace else."

"See? You think you've got him back, so you don't need me anymore."

She threw her hands up in the air. "No! I'm just not going to sit around and listen to you make comments like that. If you're not mature enough to handle the situation—"

"Here," I said, reaching into my back pocket and pulling out some cash. "Here's my immature part of the rent."

"Keep it," she said.

"Did you get a raise?"

"No," she said, getting out some plates. "Alessandro and I will cover rent from now on."

I rolled my eyes. "Then I'll just keep this," I said, putting it back in my pocket, "till next week or so when he leaves again."

Almost on cue, the front door opened. "Tiff, I couldn't find the sub shop you wanted, so I—oh, hi, Sandrino," he said, seeing me. "Glad you are back."

"Sandro," I said. "If you must talk to me, call me Sandro."

"Sorry," he muttered, putting the two brown bags on the kitchen table.

"What'd you bring?" Mom asked.

"Chinese," he said, lifting the little white containers out. "I seem to remember eating Chinese with you." He pulled her into his arms. "And you liked the Kung Pao shrimp."

"Sure hope you brought something else," I said, peering into the other bag. "She's allergic to all shellfish."

He pulled back from her. "No!"

She nodded.

"Are you sure?" he asked her. "Can you just try one? For me?"

"Feel like spending a romantic night in the hospital, do you?" I asked.

"Sandro, that's enough!" Mom snapped. Then she turned back to Alessandro. "Did you bring anything else?" she asked.

"Well, yes. I purchased sweet and sour pork and sesame chicken, but I brought a double order of the shrimp."

"Guess that's what you're eating then," I said, locating the chicken.

"You don't like shrimp, either?"

"Heredity," I said. "I've known the cause of half of my allergies." Then I grinned. "But Mom always said I got my thick skull and irritating habits from you."

"Any habits you received from me are endearing. If they're irritating, you must be doing them wrong."

I plopped down in front of the TV with the little white carton and a fork.

"What are you doing?" Alessandro said.

"Eating."

"You don't get all of the chicken."

"Why not?" I asked as I picked up the remote and began flipping through channels.

"Because we're all supposed to share all of the dishes."

"Mom and I can't eat the shrimp," I reminded him. "And I don't like pork. So that just leaves the chicken."

"But then—" he broke off. "Fine. Never mind. You get the chicken, I get the shrimp, and Tiffany gets the pork."

Mom smiled at him. "Sweet and sour pork is one of my favorites," she said.

"Liar," I muttered under my breath. I knew Mom hated pork as much as I did, but I wasn't going to offer to share the chicken. I was hungry, and it wasn't my fault Alessandro didn't know anything about us.

Alessandro cleared his throat. "Could we at least eat off plates? And sit at the table together? As a family?"

"Why?" I asked. "It just means someone's got to do dishes."

"I'll do the dishes," Alessandro said.

"Sure," Mom said, taking the remote out of my hand and turning the TV off. "We're going to eat dinner together."

"But I was watching—"

"Now, Sandro," Mom said, pulling the carton of chicken out of my hand and taking it to the table.

Sighing, I stood up. By the time I got to the table, Mom had already dished the chicken out onto all three plates. Then she put pork on everyone's plate as well.

"Fried rice?" Alessandro asked me.

"I like steamed," I said.

"Here," he said, smiling triumphantly. "I got both."

"Well, weren't you smart?"

"Sandro," Mom warned.

"Things are going to have to change around here," Alessandro announced. "And one of the first things that has to change is your attitude."

It took every ounce of willpower I had not to throw my fork in his face.

In one shining second, Mom showed more intelligence and more backbone than I thought she could ever possess. "Alessandro, becoming a family isn't going to happen overnight," she said, putting her hand over his. "Sandro is angry, and I don't think that you coming in here making demands of him is fair." Then she turned to me. "But I would like you to give him the opportunity to be part of our family."

Instead of answering, I just started eating. We ate in

silence for several minutes, but it wasn't an awkward silence.

"Why are you so angry with me, Sandrino?" I glared at him, and he quickly said, "*Sandro*. I meant to say Sandro." Sighing, he looked at Mom. "It is hard to realize I have a son who is not a *bambino*. In my dreams my son was always 'Sandrino.' It will be hard to break the habit."

"As long as you try," Mom said, glancing at me. "We're all going to have to do a lot of trying." I kept eating. "Sandro, could you try to answer Alessandro?"

"I didn't realize it was a serious question that needed an answer."

Alessandro started to talk, but Mom put her hand on his arm. "We would both like to know why you're so mad at him."

"He used you and then left us."

Alessandro took a deep breath. "I did not treat your mother with the respect she deserves, but that is because I was young and stupid."

"So that makes it all right?"

"I'm not saying what I did was all right, I'm telling you why. I had just finished my schooling at Dartmouth, and I had virtually no money. And that's why I had to borrow Tiffany's credit card."

"Whoa, whoa!" I said, holding up my hands. "You stole it from her!"

"I most certainly did not! You're making this up as you go along!"

"Okay, okay, so tell us the story of how you two met," I said.

"I thought you hated that story," Mom said.

"That's because I got sick of hearing it every day. But according to you, now I've got it all wrong. So maybe I need to hear it again. And hear *his* side, too," I said.

Sighing, Mom gave Alessandro an embarrassed grin and then cleared her throat. "Well, we met the second day of my spring-break trip."

"Right."

"And we—well, I—knew instantly that he was the man of my dreams." Alessandro picked up her hand and kissed it. "We spent the week together. He told me that he was spending some vacation time in the U.S. before going back to Italy to work, and I knew he hardly had any money."

"Okay, first lie."

"It's not a lie."

"Either you were lying when you used to tell me the story or you're lying now. One of them's got to be a lie."

"Did you ever think that maybe you don't remember the story correctly?" Mom asked in a gentle tone. Had she been sharp, I wouldn't have even given the question a second's thought. But I knew that there had been several times that I had "misremembered" something as a kid.

"He said no when I offered my father's credit card, but when he saw how big the hotel bill was . . ."

"I panicked," Alessandro said. "So I took her father's credit card and used it for the room. I was so embarrassed I left without saying anything." He picked up Mom's hand and kissed it again.

After she kissed his hand in return, she continued, "After I got back to Texas, I realized I was pregnant. I left a few messages for Alessandro, but even then I knew he might not be home for several months. I decided to move here. A few months later, his old number was disconnected—"

"My father had decided to move," Alessandro murmured. "He wanted me educated in America, yes, but he wanted me to marry good Italian girl. I hadn't heard from you and thought . . ." He spread his hands and shrugged.

"—and the letters were returned to me. So I—we—stayed here, hoping he would come find me—us."

I looked at her for a few seconds, but she seemed to think the story was done. "You moved here after your dad kicked you out, right?"

"No," Mom said, blinking. "I moved out before he and Mom even knew I was pregnant. I didn't want to disappoint them."

"But they know now, yes?" Alessandro said.

"No," Mom said, looking down at her plate.

"You've denied them their grandchild?"

"I didn't know how to tell them," Mom said. I saw a teardrop splatter on the rice. "And each year, it just got harder."

I had always thought family was overrated, mostly because my father was a thief and a liar and my grandfather was a heartless tyrant. Neither of those truths seemed to be true now. I would have to think about this.

Alessandro was frowning. "It is wrong to keep family apart, Tiffany."

"Don't tell her what to do," I said, even though I agreed with him. "You weren't here to help. She was waiting for you and you never came back."

"I didn't know she was here," he said patiently. "I called her from California once, before I went back to Italy. They told me she had run away. They didn't know how to reach her. When I got home, no one ever told me she had called, so I thought it was just a pleasant week together, that I didn't mean anything more to her. I was devastated, so I dated a lot of girls, trying to soothe my heart. I didn't find any with her sparkle, her magnetism. Then I buried myself in my work." Again he kissed her hand. "But I never forgot you."

"I think I'm gonna puke," I muttered.

Alessandro looked me in the eye. "I never left you. I didn't know. And that's neither your mother's nor my fault."

"Then whose fault was it?"

"It would be nice if there was always someone to blame, wouldn't it? But there is not. It was meant to be, for whatever reason. I suppose it was our destiny."

"You believe that crap, too?"

"We're back together," he said, smiling at Mom in such a way that I felt like I should leave the room. "And I feel like we've never been apart."

"If I hadn't come looking for Sandro, if I had been five minutes earlier or later, we would have missed each other again," Mom murmured.

"No," he said, touching her cheek. "We would have found each other somehow, somewhere."

"I just ate!" I complained.

Mom turned to me. "That reminds me. Do you know *why* I came to see you yesterday?"

"Thought you were looking for rent," I said, shrugging. Then I couldn't take the hurt look on her face. She had never asked me for rent; I just knew she had a hard time making it some months, so I helped out as much as I could. "Why *did* you come looking for me?"

"Mr. Risty came to talk to me."

I groaned and pushed back from the table, taking my plate to the sink. "No, Mom."

"Why not?" she demanded.

"Who is this Mr. Risty?" Alessandro interjected.

When I didn't say anything, Mom said, "The ski coach."

"What's your best event?" he asked.

"I don't ski on the team."

"Why not?"

"That's what I wanted to talk to him about," Mom cut in. "Risty wants to know why you're not on the team. I thought you said you didn't make the team."

"I didn't." Under her stare, I squirmed a little. "You can't make the team when you don't try out," I muttered.

"Why didn't you try out?"

"I've got better things to do."

"Like what?" Alessandro wanted to know.

"Like working."

"Risty says you've got Olympic potential," Mom said.

"Of course, he does! It's in the blood!" Alessandro proclaimed.

"Risty's an idiot," I snapped. "He's only seen me ski once. He has no idea what my potential is."

"He wants you on the team. So much that he came looking for me, asking what kind of financial help would get you on the team. And, by the way, I wish you'd quit acting like I starve you."

"You may not starve me," I said, "but you can't pretend our cupboards are overflowing."

Mom rolled her eyes at me. "Risty came to see me," she repeated. "Why would he do that if he didn't really think you were really good?"

"Because he thinks dangling the Olympics in front of me will make me want to join the team."

"And it doesn't?"

I shook my head. "It takes years of training to go to the Olympics, Mom."

"Unless you're a natural."

"Which you are," Alessandro said. "Scarpettarinis have been famous skiers for generations. Skiing is in our blood."

"Must have skipped a generation, huh?"

"Sandro!" Mom exclaimed.

Ignoring Mom, Alessandro said, "The only thing you should be doing is skiing. I always dreamed of having a son to take our name to Olympic glory."

"Then go knock someone else up," I said, walking toward my room. "And this time, stick around long enough to give the kid your last name."

"That's enough!" Alessandro roared. "I will not have you throw that in my face every time we talk! I didn't know! But I know *now*, and I'm staying *now*. So you'd better learn to deal with it." He wasn't shouting anymore. "Things are going to change around here, Sandro, so you'd better grow up."

Before I could retort, Mom cut in smoothly. "One of the things that will be changing is that we'll have more money."

"Good for you," I said tiredly.

"Good for *you*," she corrected. "You don't have to work anymore. You can be on the team instead."

"No, thanks." And as she opened her mouth to say something, I said, "Really, Mom, I should go study now." I shot a look at Alessandro. "I've had enough excitement today, and I need to go to school tomorrow."

I pushed my bedroom door shut and just stood there for a few moments, leaning my head against it. I could hear them, but I couldn't make out the words. They both sounded angry. After a few minutes, I heard the front door slam shut.

Sighing, I walked over to my desk and looked at my books. Schoolwork had never bothered me. But tonight, I just wasn't up to reading about Holden Caulfield or working out any theorems.

I had just flopped down on my bed when there was a knock on my door. Before I could say anything, it slowly opened.

"Can I come in?" Mom asked.

"I thought you left."

"Alessandro went out."

"He just can't handle it when things get hot, can he?"

"I asked him to leave," she said, "so he could calm down and I could talk to you."

"Mom, there's not much to talk about."

She sat down on the edge of my bed. "I disagree."

I looked up at the ceiling and shook my head. "Maybe there's stuff to talk about, but it's not going to do anybody any good. It's just going to get everyone upset."

"We've got to work through this."

"Why?"

She blinked. "What do you mean 'why'?"

"Why? Why do we have to work through this? Why can't we just pretend we never saw him?"

"I love him, Sandro."

"You don't even know him! You barely even knew him when I was conceived. It was just lust then. Now it's hanging on to something you *thought* you had."

"I loved him when you were conceived, and I love him now. Haven't you heard about love at first sight?"

"Oh, please."

She looked at me with her bright blue eyes. "I don't know how you got so cynical. But I'm a romantic." She gave me a little smile. "Always have been. And I'm tired of being alone."

"So I have to suffer."

"He's your father."

I slammed my fist into the wall. "That's not my fault, and that's not the point!"

"Then what is the point?"

"The point is, why are you setting us up for this?"

"Setting us up for what?" she asked in bewilderment.

"For disappointment. We know he'll leave us again."

"You don't know that. And I'm pretty sure he won't leave us."

For some reason I felt the burning of tears in my eyes. All I could do was shake my head. Unfortunately, that shook a couple of tears loose. Mom wiped my cheek, and I jerked away from her.

She sighed. "Okay, you're right. Talking about this isn't going to get us anywhere."

"Thank you," I said, after I cleared my throat.

"So let's talk about the ski team."

"Mom!"

"Do you dislike skiing?"

"Don't be stupid."

"Don't get sassy," Mom snapped back. "If you're not going to make this easy, then I'll take it one step at a time. So," she repeated, "do you dislike skiing?"

"No."

"Are you good at it?"

"Mom—"

"We haven't gone skiing together since you were little, so I don't know. You used to be very good."

"I'm good."

"And I know you've got the grades to be on a team."

"Yeah."

"So what's stopping you?"

"Do you have any idea how much it will take to be on the team?" I asked her, staring up at the ceiling.

"What do you mean?"

"They practice over at Alpine, three days a week. The other two days, they're doing weights, running, and reviewing films."

"For someone who's not on the team, you know an awful lot about it," she observed.

"And there's a race almost every week."

"So?"

"So I won't be able to work."

"You won't need to—"

"If I'm not working," I continued, "then I'm not going to be able to help with rent—"

"You don't need to worry about that," she said quickly.

"I won't be able to pay for the team jacket, the transportation, let alone getting the decent equipment I'll need."

"We'll help."

"Mom, you can't—"

"Sandro, do you want to ski on the team? I really want to know."

"Yeah," I said, feeling like I was betraying someone. "I think it'd be cool. But—"

"Stop," she said, holding up her hand. "Stop right there. If you want to be on the team, then go see Mr. Risty tomorrow at school. We'll figure out the details after that."

"Okay."

She smiled at me, and then suddenly leaned forward and kissed me on the forehead. "Good night, Sandro."

"Good night, Mom."

She left, and I just lay there, thinking. Somehow my world was changing. It was like I was stuck in a fairy-tale teen movie. These things didn't happen to people. I spent the rest of the night trying to figure out what I would do when it all started to fall apart.

8

When my alarm clock went off the next morning, all I wanted to do was throw it out the window. I had hardly slept at all. But I got up, got ready, and gathered my stuff as quietly as I could. I absolutely did not want to run into Alessandro.

At the bus stop, I said hi to Jamie and the other kids who lived in the resort apartments; then I started the reading I should have done the night before. By the time we pulled up to the school, I was almost done with the chapter.

"Hey, Sandro!"

"Hey, LeMoyne," I said as he fell in step with me in the hall. "How's it going?"

"Rather hear how you're doing."

"Why's that?"

"First your dad shows up, then you bail at work, then yesterday you don't even show up for school. I think you've got more to talk about."

I dropped my backpack by my locker. "Not really. Did I miss anything yesterday?"

"Nah, man. Just same ol' same ol'."

"Cool."

"You're really not going to tell me what happened?"

"It seems that Daddy's home," I said, shrugging. "And they say I've got to join the ski team."

"Really? You gonna talk to Risty?"

"Yep," I said, shutting my locker. "Right now."

"A'aight. Then I'll catch you in English."

"You don't want to come see Risty?"

"Nah, man. Later," he said, turning to walk away.

I watched him disappear in the crowd before I turned to go to the gym. Damn it, I should have thought before talking. LeMoyne had been working hard to make the team, and I was going to walk on without a question.

Our school only had about fifteen guys and fifteen girls on the ski team each year, but at most of the races, only ten could compete. There were ten meets in the season, each at a different school's home mountain. The resorts didn't want to tie up their slopes all day with high schoolers when there were tourists who were willing to pay extra money for the racecourses.

I had grown up with about half of the kids in my school; the other half had moved in later, like LeMoyne. The kids who had grown up here had been skiing all their lives, like me, but not many of them were as good as I was. I wished I could explain why I was so good, but I couldn't. It just happened. I could ski—and jump—almost anything.

Mr. Risty's office door was open. I walked in without looking, and once again found myself regretting my confidence.

"Hi, Sandro," Mr. Risty said in surprise. "What happened to your face?"

"Nothing."

"Are you okay?"

"I'm fine. Don't worry about it."

"We were just talking about you. I think you know Phil."

I nodded at Sirocco. "Yeah. We know each other."

"He said there was a race this weekend."

"Unofficial," I said.

"Very," Sirocco agreed.

"Phil has the same opinion your boss and LeMoyne do," Mr. Risty said. "You've got a lot of people trying to get you on this team."

I glanced at Sirocco in surprise. He was staring at Risty and ignoring me.

"I thought the team was full," I said carefully.

Mr. Risty frowned. "It is, in a manner of speaking. Practices started two weeks ago, and we just had our first time trial last week. Usually, we cut at the first time trials and only take the top fifteen racers. But two people who made the team came out positive for the drug test, and six more had drops in grades so are no longer eligible." He hesitated. "And as I'm sure you know, the team hasn't done very well the last couple of years."

"Last year, we only won one meet, and only had four people qualify for State," Sirocco said in disgust.

"We're going to have another time trial tomorrow," Mr. Risty said. "There was only two seconds' difference between twelfth and eighteenth last week. I want to make sure we get the best racers, not just a couple of flukes."

"So if I were able to place in the top fifteen tomorrow—"

"You have to be eligible and have your permission form turned in, and you have to be at practice today."

"Okay," I said slowly. "I think I can do all that."

"Good," Mr. Risty said, smiling. "Then we'll see you at practice. Four o'clock at Alpine."

"Okay," I said, hoping I could make the bus in time.

"What changed your mind, Sandro?"

I shook my head. "Guess I'm giving into peer pressure."

"Did your mom talk to you?"

"Yeah."

"Sorry I had to do that."

"I guess it just shows how much you want me on the team." I didn't bother to tell him that talking to Mom wouldn't have made a difference a few days ago.

The bell rang. Sirocco stood up.

"See you both this afternoon," Risty said as Sirocco and I left his office.

Once we were in the hall, I reached into my back pocket. "Here," I said, holding my hand out to Sirocco.

"What's that?"

"Our bet."

He waved his hand. "Keep it. You need it more than I do."

"I pay my bets," I said, still holding the cash out to him.

He rolled his eyes. "I'm sure you do. But I'm not going to worry about taking food off your table." And he turned and walked away before I could say anything else.

I couldn't think about Sirocco and his cockiness because I had too much make-up work to do. LeMoyne was able to help me out in English and calculus, and the only class that had given a pop quiz turned out to be Spanish.

"You going to Alpine tomorrow for the time trial?" I asked LeMoyne as the last bell rang.

"I don't think so."

"Why not?"

"I ain't got the stuff," he said, shaking his head.

"What are you talking about?"

"I placed seventeenth at the time trials, man. And with you steppin' in, I'd be lucky to stay at seventeen instead of being bumped even further back."

"You could move up. Make top fifteen."

He was shaking his head. "I don't think so. You totally dusted me on Saturday—"

"So? There are fifteen places on the team. Besides, maybe you'll have the run of your life tomorrow."

LeMoyne just kept shaking his head.

"Come on, man, don't make me go out there alone."

His eyebrows went up. "You made me go out there alone for the last two weeks!"

"So now you quit? How does that make me feel?"

"It ain't you," he said, leaning back against the locker. "It's just reality bitin' me in the butt. I ain't got the stuff. Wish I did, but I don't."

"I don't buy it," I said flatly. "You were gung ho this weekend. Hell, you were on my case this weekend. And now that I'm tryin' out, you're quittin'. How can I possibly *not* think it's me?"

"Sirocco's got it all wrapped up."

"What?"

"He's got it all wrapped up. His buddies are all on the team," LeMoyne said. "They've got the ten top spots, and those are the only ones that really get to race anyway."

"Then why would he want me on the team?"

"Because his friends suck, and he knows it."

"They're really tight, huh?"

"He wants to win. It's more important than friends."

I shut my locker. "Friends are more important," I said. "Give it one more shot tomorrow. We'll practice today and see what we can do for you."

"I'm a lost cause."

"We'll find you," I said, putting my arm around his shoulders and pushing him down the hall.

"Yeah? Where are we gonna start looking?"

"At the shop. We gotta go get our skis."

- - -

"Go-go-go-go!" I shouted. "Work it! Move-move-mo— Oh crap!" I watched in dismay as LeMoyne missed a cut on the gate, his skis went clattering, and he fell off the course.

"Aarghh!"

"You all right?" I called up to him.

His arm waved back and forth and then fell back down.

I leaned forward on my poles and waited, watching as the next skier came down. I thought it was Alan Webster, one of Sirocco's pals. He was good, but he was a little too tense. His knees weren't loose enough to give and take with the mountain's curves. In fact, he skied a lot like—

"LeMoyne!" I hollered. "Get down here!"

He finished brushing himself off and came down the side toward me. We were just off the course, staying out of everyone's way, but close enough to hear them grunt as they whipped past.

"Let's go," I said, turning down the hill right before he reached me.

"Wait up, man!"

"It's training, LeMoyne! Catch me if you can!"

I went barreling down the slope, knees bending and bouncing over each of the moguls, twisting at the waist and keeping my shoulders and head perfectly still.

Spraying snow everywhere, I pulled to a stop in front of the lift.

"Last run!" Mr. Risty was calling on his bullhorn. "Last run!"

I looked back up the mountain. LeMoyne had fallen behind me quite a bit. The mountain was quiet because we were the only ones allowed on this run during practice time. Looking up the slalom course, I could see the team hopefuls at various points. Overall, I wasn't impressed.

LeMoyne caught up. Before he slowed down, I was moving toward the lift. "Come on, man," I said. "We only get one more run."

We got on the chair, and I started telling LeMoyne about his run and what I thought he could do to improve. We got into the discussion, and neither of us was really ready to get off the chair.

"Okay," LeMoyne nodded as we slid over to the start-ing gate. "You really think just having fun will make me go faster?"

"Yeah," I said. "You're trying too hard, and it's just getting in the way. Relax. Let your knees move. And remember to cut the turns *before* you get to the gate. If you cut them when you get there, it's too late to make it tight."

"Got it," he said. Then he flashed me a big grin. "I'm pumped!"

I had to grin back. "Then go!"

He got in the starting gate, and I stayed off to the side, hearing the countdown tones to the final buzzer. He was slow from the gate, I observed. He'd have to practice jumps at home tonight—get ready to explode from the gate instead of just pushing out of it.

But he looked good going into the turns. He disappeared over the ridge, and I was smiling to myself. He had found his groove.

"You aren't on the team yet." I looked up to see Sirocco and Webster standing behind me. "And if you're this slow gettin' into the gate, you're gonna get run over before you even leave it."

When I didn't say anything, Alan Webster said, "Are you going or what?"

"Go ahead," I said, still looking down at the mountain.

Webster adjusted his goggles and slid into the gate. Sirocco slid over next to me. We listened to the countdown. Webster leaped out of the gate, charging down the slope.

As he went over the ridge, I said, "He's not bad."

"No. Not bad. But not great, either. No one on this team can even push me. That's why I need you."

"If you need someone else to push you, you're not gonna get far."

"I like to rise to the challenge. I'll get as far as I want."

"How about just getting down the hill?" I asked.

"After you," he said.

"I'll see you on the bus," I said.

"Only if you blink when I pass you."

I shook my head and slid into the gate. As the countdown started, I could actually feel my heart speed up. If my heart got a head start, it could usually keep up with my body down the mountain. My stomach, however, usually clenched up and felt like lead. I liked to think that the extra weight would help me gain speed.

As the final tone sounded, I launched myself out of the gate. My skis were quick and responsive, cutting around the gates with the precision of an Exacto knife.

The top ridge had enough lift to catch some air. Strictly speaking, as a slalom skier, too much air could slow you down. But I had had a good day, and I wanted to play. I pulled a quick back-scratcher and landed just a little off the ideal line. It took a few gates to get back in the right line, and by that time, I could see Webster in front of me.

I only had time to register that Webster was slowing down on the course before I was almost on top of him. Yelling, I let myself miss the next gate, swinging wide and bumping awkwardly over two moguls before getting back in control.

Skidding to a stop, I turned and shouted, "What the hell are you thinking, Webster?"

The words were hardly out of my mouth before he doubled over and fell.

Cursing, I popped out of my skis and began clumsily climbing up to Webster. Out of the corner of my eye, I saw Sirocco speeding through the gates.

"Stop!" I bellowed. "Man down! Man down!"

Just as I was sure Sirocco was going to plow right into him, he somehow managed to swerve and barely clip Webster's skis instead.

I kept making my way up to Webster. Sirocco went careening off the course with even less grace than I had shown. He bumped over three moguls in a row and then went down with a yell, going over the ridge and disappearing from sight.

Webster was groaning.

"What's wrong, man?"

He groaned again. I knelt beside him in the snow. "Can you hear me, Alan?"

"Yeah."

"What happened? What's wrong?"

"My stomach," he gasped. "I think I'm gonna—" I jumped out of the way, which was good because he finished the thought with action instead of words.

Meanwhile, Sirocco was yelling curses, which were, for some reason, directed at me.

The comforting sound of an approaching snowmobile reached me. "Here!" I yelled, standing up and waving because it gave me something to do. "Over here!"

The ski patrol got off his snowmobile and began walking toward us. Over his shoulder, I saw Sirocco climbing up out of the trees. He was okay.

Other than explaining what I had seen, there wasn't much I could do. I put my skis back on and headed down the mountain, waving when the ski patrol passed me by.

- - -

At school, we learned that Webster had mono. It messed with his spleen, which had ruptured. He had gone from the mountain to the hospital, and straight in for surgery. Sirocco had gone directly to the team trainers, whining about his knee, and getting everyone to pity him, virtually discounting Webster's condition.

LeMoyne had been upset I hadn't seen his run, but when he saw ski patrol coming down, he got over it. I had talked to him about his start, and he went home swearing to practice all night. I suggested that he try to get at least a little sleep.

I don't think he got any, but he looked pretty good on the only practice run we got the next day.

"I can't do this. . . . I can't do this," LeMoyne kept saying for almost the entire chairlift up. I was sick of telling him he could, so I just ignored him.

We got off the lift and skied over to the gates with everyone else. There were fifty people there waiting to race, hoping to make one of the thirty-four spots on the team. Risty had announced last night that he would keep seventeen boys and seventeen girls, but had emphasized that, at most meets, only the top ten of each would be skiing.

That was fine with LeMoyne. He just wanted to be on the team. And he was terrified he would fall or go even slower than he had last week.

I had never been nervous about starting before. But standing there, watching everyone else stretch and do breathing exercises and talk quietly, it started to get to me. I was pretty sure I'd make the cut; in fact, I was pretty sure I'd be in the top five without much effort, but the tension was almost contagious.

Risty told us we'd be going alphabetically, so I worked my way over to the gate. I was glad LeMoyne's last name was Marshall. Staying close to him would give me a headache.

Sasha Anderson and Missy Barton were standing in front of me, talking quietly. Mike Alexander was already in the gate, which meant we were starting very soon.

The countdown started, and everyone got quiet. We all shouted as Mike left the gate and headed down the slopes.

In rapid succession, Sasha and Missy followed, and it was my turn to go. I think everyone shouted for me when I launched, but I really wasn't paying attention. Instead, I was throwing my whole body into the race, reaching for the first gate.

I had a clean run and the fastest one so far. Mr. Risty was writing times and notes down at the bottom of the run, but all he did was give me a thumbs up. Mike and Sasha both congratulated me on my time. I, however, wasn't pleased.

I had known, of course, that being in the front of the run meant I had to wait for the results, but I hadn't *really* known what that meant. It would take the better part of two hours for everyone else to finish. The thought of sitting around that long was not appealing.

With a sigh, I took off my skis and sat on a bench. What I wanted to do most was get on a chairlift and do a few runs. But I needed to wait until LeMoyne was down. I owed him at least that much.

One by one, the rest of the hopefuls maneuvered through the gates. My time stood the test, but that didn't make it any easier to sit and watch.

Finally, LeMoyne came down the course. I only had a clear view of the bottom third of the course, but from what I could see, he was running the line he needed. He was cutting the gates cleanly, but if he wanted to drop time, he needed to be more aggressive.

LeMoyne crossed the finish line, with the tenth-fastest time as far as I knew. I had no idea how that was split between the boys and the girls, though, and there were at least twenty more skiers to go, including Sirocco. LeMoyne was going to be right on the edge of the cutoff; which side of that edge, I didn't know.

I popped back into my skis and waved LeMoyne over to the lift.

"Where're you goin'?" he said.

"Thought I'd do somethin' crazy and ski. You comin'?"

He hesitated. "What about the results?"

I shrugged. "They'll be available when we get back. Accurate and complete."

"Let's go," he said, skiing in front of me into the line.

Once in the chair, he leaned back. "How'd we do?"

I shook my head. "Let's just have fun this afternoon, okay?"

He laughed. "You sound like you've been working hard on your skiing for years, and not letting it be fun 'stead of the other way around."

"The day skiing isn't fun is the day I give away my boots," I agreed. "But that doesn't mean I haven't worked at it. I don't want to think about the race right now. It won't do us any good to stress."

"You're right. But saying you don't *want* to stress and *not* stressing are two totally different things."

He was right, but I wasn't about to admit it.

We skied three runs, taking our time and doing more jumps than anything else. We laughed at each other; we talked about the girl LeMoyne wanted to ask out; we talked about people at the shop; we talked about everything but the time trial. But the trial was the only thing we were thinking about.

As we got closer to the base, I felt my stomach tightening up. I was still sure—mostly—that I had made the team. I was worried about LeMoyne. At least that's what I kept telling myself.

We got to the bottom of the course in time to see the last three skiers come down. None of them beat my time; one of them was faster than LeMoyne.

Everyone began filing toward the team room as the last skier removed her skis. Mr. Risty was still scribbling furiously on his clipboard, and his assistant had just skied down from her vantage point in the middle of the run.

I thought the tension had been bad before the time trial, but that was nothing next to the tension in the team room. Several of the girls appeared close to tears, and a couple of the guys were sitting with arms crossed and scowls on their faces. I assumed they were at the bottom of the results.

Sirocco and his group of buddies were overly casual in their stances and far too loud compared to everyone else. LeMoyne muttered something about Sirocco's smug grin, but I was recognizing it for what it was. Sirocco was good, and he knew it. That was fine. What he didn't need to do, though, was laugh about others' times while they were in the room.

"All right, folks," Mr. Risty said as he came in the room, quieting us down immediately. "I will post the list in just a few moments. I don't think the results will be any big surprises for most of you. I am reserving a spot on the team for Alan Webster, even though he didn't race today. I took his time from last week, and it placed him fourth overall among the boys. You are ranked by time from one to twenty-three for the girls and one to twenty-seven for the boys."

He paused and cleared his throat before continuing, "Those of you who made the team are expected to be at all practices, whether on the mountain, in the weight room, or on the track. You're also to maintain your grades. If I have to pull you from a practice and put you in a study hall, I'll do it in a heartbeat. Any questions?"

Nobody said anything. I couldn't believe he was making

us wait to see the list instead of just reading it out to us. Finally, he nodded.

"See you tomorrow," he said, and he walked out the door, stopping just long enough to tack the list up on the wall by the door.

There was a split-second pause, and then most of the people in the room bolted for the list. I wasn't in a hurry. Neither was LeMoyne. At first, I was surprised, but then he began his chant, "I can't look. . . . I can't look. . . . I can't look—"

I groaned. As the room emptied, I stood up. "Let's go see."

"I can't, man. I really can't."

"Come on," I said.

He shook his head and actually grabbed on to the legs of the chair he was sitting on.

"Fine," I said.

I walked over, sure that the pounding of my heart was only because I was worried for LeMoyne.

I started at the bottom of the boys' list and began moving up. "Sixteen, LeMoyne Marshall."

I turned and looked over my shoulder at him. "Sixteen, LeMoyne! You made it!"

Slowly, he lifted his head. "No, it's the top—"

"Seventeen," I said. "Risty said he was taking the top seventeen this year, even though—" I stopped myself and then continued, "he's taking top seventeen instead of fifteen this year. You're on the team, man!"

"You sure?"

"I'm positive!"

LeMoyne finally got up and let out a big "Whooop!" and practically danced over to me. He wrapped me in a bear hug, and then let go abruptly, turning to the list. "Let me see, let me see," he said, running his finger along the numbers.

"You don't think I'd lie to you?"

"Sixteen! Sweet sixteen!" And he started to dance again.

I had to laugh. He was so excited that he barely made the team, I certainly couldn't tell him how I felt about finishing second behind Sirocco again.

9

"Aahh," I sighed, dropping my backpack on the living room floor. Rolling my shoulders, I pushed the door shut and then headed toward my room. Practice had been long again tonight, and my only chance of staying awake to finish my homework was to take a good thirty-minute nap. Hopefully, I'd wake up.

I had just flopped down on my bed when I heard the front door open again. Then I made the mistake of looking over my shoulder to see if I had shut my bedroom door. It was still wide open, and Alessandro was standing in it.

He made a great show of looking at his Rolex. "Going to bed at eight? That's too early, even for a school night."

I put my head down on my pillow. Somehow, he took that as an invitation to come in.

"What's wrong?" he asked. "Are you sick?"

"Of you," I muttered into the pillow.

"What?"

I pushed myself up on my elbows. "I'm just really tired. After a catnap, I'll be able to function, okay?"

Alessandro sat down. "You look beat."

"That's what I just said."

"You have too much stress in your life."

Raising my eyebrows, I said, "Thanks to you."

"Your face is healing."

"Yes." I thought that the removal of the stitches and the fact that the bruise was almost gone made that obvious.

"Come," he said. "Let's have a beer."

I watched in disbelief as he stood up and headed toward the kitchen. I thought of staying where I was, but I knew he'd just come back. I didn't want him to get comfortable hanging out in my room.

By the time I had finally pulled myself off the bed and into the living room, he had already popped the lids off two bottles. It was too late to tell him I didn't want one. All beer seemed to do was either exhaust me or make me pee a lot.

"Cheers," he said, clinking bottle necks with me. I took a small sip while he drained half his bottle.

"So."

I stared at him. "What?"

"Tell me everything."

"You're kidding, right?"

"No. I'm very serious. I want to know all about my son."

My skin almost crawled hearing him say that. "Maybe I want to know about you," I said, trying not to gag.

He spread his hands. "What do you want to know?"

"Why are you here?"

It was his turn to stare. "What do you mean?"

"Why now? What brought you back to Borealis *now*?"

"I wanted to retrace my footsteps."

"But why now?" I pressed. "Why didn't you do it for a ten- or even fifteen-year anniversary trip or something? What's so special about the almost eighteen-year mark?"

"There have been some problems."

I waited while he drank some more beer, but then he didn't say anything else. "What kind of problems?" I asked, even while I was suspecting it had something to do with alcohol.

"Family problems." He killed the bottle and then stood up. Holding up his bottle toward me, he raised his eyebrows, and I shook my head.

"You and your wife start counseling or something?" I asked.

"Hah!" he said, closing the fridge. "I see what you think. I never got married. No, the problems were with my father and brother."

"Oh?"

"We had a family olive oil business. My father, he ran it like an army. He paid for college and then my brother and I were automatically enlisted. This was okay for a while, but after a few years, my younger brother hated it. He and my father fought, and he ran away."

"What's your brother's name?"

"Mario."

Uncle Mario, I thought, testing the idea. "What did he hate about it?"

"Everything. Mostly just being under my father's thumb." Alessandro sighed. "Mario came back, needing money. My father, he was very ill. It was my turn to fight with Mario. I hated that he only came back for the money, that he expected to be taken in again as if he had done nothing wrong. My father's last wish was that Mario and I make peace."

"Your father died?"

"Your grandfather died two months ago."

"And you and Mario buried the hatchet?" Alessandro gave me a funny look. Using his words, I said, "You made peace?"

"No. My father left the business to both of us, to force us to talk, trying to control us from the grave. Instead, I came here. Mario can learn how hard it is to run a business. Let him see what my father and I were doing while he was out being a playboy. I never got a chance to decide what I wanted to do with my life because I obeyed my father in all things. I never did anything without his permission."

I almost pointed out that Alessandro had already done his share of being a playboy, a little more than seventeen years ago, but decided against it. "So you're just here to have your midlife crisis."

He glanced at me. "In a way, yes."

I set my still-full beer down on the table and stood up.

"Where are you going?"

"To do my homework," I said, although I was pretty sure I wouldn't be able to keep my eyes open that long.

"Sit," he insisted. "Talk to me. Let's get to know each other."

"Let's not," I said. "Besides, I've got to keep my grades up if I'm going to stay on the team."

"Study! Go study!" he said immediately. "Above all, you must ski."

As I turned to go to my room, I asked one more time, "Midlife crisis?"

"Yes."

"So much for destiny," I muttered as I shut my bedroom door.

- - -

"Are you kidding me? You want Sunday off *again*?"

"Come on, Kolton—"

"No," he said, shaking his head. "It's Thursday. It's too late for me to make changes."

Even though I knew it was a lost cause, I tried again, "But—"

"Find someone to cover your shift, or be here," he said, and he walked away.

"Robert—"

"I'm already working Sunday. Is this the third weekend you're trying to get out of work? Man, you're getting worse than Jade."

"I know, I know," I muttered.

"What do you need it off for, anyway?" he asked. "I thought the races were always on Fridays."

"Yeah," I said. I thought quickly then said again, "Yeah. It's cool. I need the work. It's all good."

Robert raised his eyebrows at me and went back to the repair room.

I tried to focus on my work for the rest of the day. It wasn't easy. Our first race was tomorrow, and I had been planning to work all weekend. But then Webster got tickets to a reggae concert for Sunday. He had invited me along with Sirocco and Chase Tangley.

During my break, I called Webster. "Hey, Alan, it's Birch. . . . I can't make it on Sunday. Why don't you give LeMoyne a call? . . . Yeah, he'd love to go. . . . Thanks for inviting me. . . . See ya tomorrow."

I hung up and when I turned around, I almost ran right over Kolton. "Whoa. You're sneakier than a cat," I said, moving around him.

"So what's up?"

"Hmm?"

"These last three weeks, you haven't been employee of the month material. In fact, you've been so bad there's no way you can catch up in the last week."

"I'm sorry, man," I said.

"So what's up?"

I was smiling like an idiot. "It's weird."

"What's weird?"

"I'm in. I've been in this town my whole life, and no one ever gave a damn. But now, everyone knows who I am, everyone wants me at their parties—"

Kolton was smiling at me. "You got big-man-on-mountain syndrome. I thought you didn't want to be the skier star."

"I didn't know what I was missing."

"Yep," Kolton sighed. "I couldn't get you to listen to me before, so I ain't gonna waste my time now. Just be careful, man."

- - -

Our first competition was at Vail, and it would be a slalom race. The coaches would seed us in order from fastest to slowest for the first run, and then the order was reversed for the second run. The events were decided by the total time of both runs. There were ten schools competing, and each team had been limited to ten male and ten female skiers. That still left two hundred skiers, and made for a very long day.

Sirocco was the first male skier from our team, and I was the second, so we rode up the chairlift together. Although I had somehow become a part of their group, Alan Webster and Chase Tangley were the only ones who had genuinely accepted me. Sirocco included me because he wanted me on the team. I was a skier of his caliber, and that was all. It didn't make us buddies.

I don't remember ever being anxious on a chairlift before that ride. Instinctively, I reached for my inside coat pocket.

Nothing was there. Smoking was against school and team policy, so I hadn't brought my pack with me. Besides, I needed to cut back before it started to affect my performance.

Sirocco sneered as he reached into his own pocket and pulled out a cigarette.

"Can I bum one?" I asked as he lit up.

"Only got the one," he said. "Sorry."

I didn't believe him, but I wasn't going to argue—or beg. Instead, I just let my anger simmer.

We rode the rest of the way in silence. As we slid off the chair and headed to the gate, I experienced a whole new feeling—terror. I was suddenly terrified of everything I was about to do. It was something that was as natural to me as breathing, but this time it meant something. I had rarely raced with anything more important than a six-pack on the line. And even now, part of my brain was telling me that there wasn't anything on the line.

It's my first time racing in front of an audience, the nervous side of my brain argued.

A high-school audience, the other part countered. *There won't even be twenty people watching at the bottom.*

While my brain went on arguing with itself, my heart was pounding, my stomach was threatening to revolt, and even my knees were shaking. I was a mess.

In the last three weeks, I had improved my overall standing on the team, but one goal still eluded me. I had yet to beat Sirocco. LeMoyne kept telling me that it was because of my skis. He was convinced that if I got the new, shorter skis, my time would drop, and I would leave Sirocco to eat my powder.

Our team alternated with the other teams for starting positions, so although I was second for our team, I would actually be starting eleventh overall. After the first run, though, we would be seeded based solely on our times.

There were shouts and yells as the buzzer counted down for Sirocco, and it was noisy until he disappeared around the bend in the course. Then it got quiet. It was too quiet for me, and I wanted to do something to break the tension. I thought about singing an old movie song, but when I opened my mouth, I threw up.

I had no idea it was coming, and I actually got some on

my skis. I was mortified, which should have gotten me over my nerves, but it didn't. I tried to cover up the stain with some snow, and I chewed on a snowball to try to get the taste out of my mouth.

"Hey! Sandro! You're up!" Mrs. Webster, the starter for the day, called.

For one horrible second, I thought I was going to throw up again. I swallowed hard, and forced myself over to the starting gate.

Once inside, I looked over to Mrs. Webster. She smiled and gave me a big thumbs-up, and then the countdown tones began. When you race by yourself, you can leave the gate as soon as you're ready. You get to decide when you've got all your momentum together.

My start was a little slow. I cut my first two gates too early, and then I barely made my third one. My rhythm was totally off.

When I caught an edge coming around the fourth gate and almost fell down, I finally got pissed. And that's when I was able to pull myself back together.

I finished the rest of the run cleanly, but I knew my time wouldn't be close to Sirocco's. I had dug myself a hole for the second run. Stepping out of my bindings, I tried to keep my cursing at a low volume. The coaches and assistants were all close by, and I didn't want to get in trouble for poor sportsmanship.

Risty tried to wave me over to him, but I knew exactly what he'd have to say. He had given me plenty of tips in the last weeks, and they all worked, but I knew what had gone wrong with my race. Nothing he would say could fix it.

So I put my skis up in the rack and walked into the lodge. Today I had to play the waiting game; Risty had been clear that he expected everyone to stick around and cheer one another on. Skiing on our own was not an option. Since school meets were on school days, we weren't supposed to be out playing.

I found Sirocco and Webster sitting at a table. Alan had just started practicing again last week and wouldn't be allowed to compete until next week at the earliest. He was the only nonskiing teammate here, and that was only because his mom was working the meet.

"Nice run," Alan said as I sat down.

"Thanks," I said.

"Chase is next," Sirocco said, almost to himself. "And once he gets down here, we'll move to a back table and play some cards."

"Sounds good," Alan said. He glanced at me. "You in, Sandro?"

"Nah. I think I'll play cheerleader."

"He means he can't afford it," Sirocco said.

Alan glanced at me. "I'll spot you."

"No thanks."

"You sure?" Alan pressed.

"Let it go," Sirocco said. "He doesn't like charity."

"But—" suddenly Webster was distracted and nodded toward the door. "Hey, Phil, looks like the poker game's off."

"Why?" Sirocco looked around. He looked back to the table and shook his head. "She must be really desperate to come all the way up here." He grinned at Webster.

"Maybe she'll show me just how desperate later."

He stood up and moved toward the door.

"We met a couple of girls in Golden last week," Webster explained. "Sirocco invited them up here. Looks like only one came."

I turned around to see Sirocco hugging a girl, then turned my attention to the slalom. Tangley was entering the last set of gates. He appeared to be on the fastest line, and I was afraid that he was going to beat my time. He tucked tight for the finish, and I looked up at the clock.

Damn. He got me by nearly one-and-a-half seconds.

"Hey, Alan, you remember Angela, right?"

"Yeah," Alan said, while I almost hurt my neck turning around too fast.

"And this is Sandro," Sirocco continued.

"Hi," Angela said.

"Hey," I said, "you got the blood out of your coat." Her fuchsia jacket looked good as new.

"Just got it back from the cleaners."

"I'd like to—"

"Don't worry about it," she said shortly.

"You two want to fill us in?" Sirocco asked.

I just looked at her, giving her the chance to tell the story the way she wanted to.

"We ran into each other—or rather someone else ran into him—on the mountain," she said lightly. "And I administered first aid."

Sirocco's eyebrows went up. "You administered first aid?"

"Yes," Angela said, seemingly unaware that he was

making fun of her. "I'm certified and—" She suddenly stopped. "I helped him. And that's how we met."

"Ah."

"Hey, Tangley!" Webster said into the awkward silence. "How's the run?"

"Not too bad," he said as he walked up to the table. He nodded toward me, "I'm sittin' fifth overall, second for our team."

"Yeah, yeah, yeah," I said, watching the next skier come down.

"You bring your wallet down the slope with you?" Sirocco asked Tangley, fiddling with Angela's hair and flipping a long lock over her shoulder.

"Poker," Webster clarified.

"Cool. Count me in," Tangley nodded.

Sirocco stood up. "Let's go."

"Where?" Angela asked.

"We're not supposed to be gambling," the ever-helpful Webster said. "So we're moving a little further out of the way. You know, out of sight."

"Oh," Angela said.

"Come on," Sirocco said, pulling on her hand. "I need to take their money before they spend it on something useless."

Angela stood up. If she didn't seem too eager, I was probably the only one who noticed.

They started to go, and I turned to watch the Vail skier entering the final stretch of the run. He made the first gate I could see, but then he caught an edge.

A lot of times, when you watch a recreational skier

wipe out, it's funny. In fact, it's not uncommon to hear the critics in the nearby chairlifts yelling things like, "Yard sale!" or "That's a nine-point-five!" But when a racer bites it, it's a very different thing.

For one thing, they're going a whole lot faster. For another, they're on hard-packed snow. In fact, sometimes the course is actually watered down the night before so it will freeze. When you wipe out on a racecourse, you walk away with bruises you can already see.

I was watching the Vail skier bounce and skid across the course. He missed the gate, but one of his poles went flying, and I didn't like the way his leg bent under him.

"That looks bad."

I glanced over. Angela was sitting down next to me. "What happened to the game?" I asked.

"I didn't come to play poker. I came to see a race."

"I thought you came to see Sirocco."

"Who?"

"Phil."

"Oh. Yeah."

"Oh yeah what?" I asked.

Instead of answering, she asked, "How was your Christmas?"

"I worked." I always did. I think I was nine when Mom and I had agreed to give each other just one gift and that was the extent of our celebration. "And yours?"

"Good," she said. "We had a family dinner and—" She broke off suddenly. "He's not moving."

"What?" I was having a hard time following her.

She nodded toward the window. "He's not moving."

As I looked back to the slope, the ski patrol began heading toward the skier. He still wasn't moving. Suddenly, I needed a smoke.

I stood up.

"Where are you going?"

I reached into my pocket. It was still empty.

"Where are you going?" she repeated.

"I need to take a walk," I said. "Want to come?"

She smiled. I think it was the first time I had seen her smile since she got here. "Yeah."

10

"So what's the story?"

"What story?"

"Why are you with Sirocco?"

She kicked a snow clod in front of her, spinning it into pieces. "Met him at a New Year's Eve party. He invited us up since our teachers had an in-service today." She shrugged.

"Us?" I asked.

"Me and a couple of friends."

"You're the only one here," I pointed out.

She flushed. "He seemed nice enough. And he's cute."

"He's loaded, too," I said.

"That's always a plus," she said in such a tone I couldn't decide if she was serious.

"You really like him?"

"I just met him," she said in exasperation. "I don't know if I really like him or not."

"But you're out here with me."

"You're not supposed to notice that," she muttered.

"Hard to get to know him when you're out here with me."

She stopped short. "If I'm bothering you, just tell me, and I'll go back inside."

"I'm sorry," I said. "I always seem to be saying the wrong things around you."

She was still just standing there. I really wanted that cigarette. Reaching down, I picked up a small stick and began twirling it between my fingers. She was watching me with a strange expression. "What?"

Angela gave herself a little shake. "Nothing." She started walking again. "Your face is looking good."

"I didn't realize you thought it was ugly before," I said lightly. She frowned at me, so I added, "It's taking a while, but it hasn't hurt at all for the last couple of weeks. I'll have a scar for the rest of my life. But that way, you know I'll never forget you."

"I'm sure scars are the only reason you'd be able to remember anything," she said dryly.

"Oh, I'd remember you even if I had amnesia."

She cleared her throat. "You didn't say anything about the ski team last time."

"You didn't stick around long enough to hear about it."

Without breaking stride, she gave me a shove.

"I'm sorry. Why do I have to keep apologizing to you?"

"Because you keep sticking your foot in your mouth."

"Yeah, but why? I'm not usually stupid."

She started to smile and tried very quickly to stop. "So about the ski team," she prodded.

"I just joined."

"The season just started, right?"

"Yeah, but this is my first year on the team."

"Why?"

"Couldn't afford it."

"And now you're loaded like Sirocco?"

"No."

"So?" she prompted.

I looked around. There was a coffee shop on the other side of the strip mall. "Come on, let's go grab something to eat."

"That didn't work so well last time."

"Let's try again and see if we can get it right," I said. "Come on."

Angela started to slip, and I reached out to catch her. "Careful!"

"Yeah, thanks."

We had taken a half-dozen steps, and she still had hold of my hand. I almost said something, but then thought better of it.

"How's your dad?" she asked.

"He's supposedly the reason I can afford the team this year."

"So he's good."

I shrugged. "I wouldn't go that far. Mom keeps saying that our situation is better since he's here."

"You don't agree?"

"She's working a lot more hours right now. And he hasn't gotten a job yet."

I pulled the door open for her. She let go of my hand and stepped inside.

We got our drinks, coffee for me and tea for her, and I also got a couple of cookies. Then we found an empty table.

"How'd you meet Sirocco?" I asked.

"At a party."

"And you drove all the way up here to see him?"

"I drove up to see a ski race."

It was on the tip of my tongue to point out that she wasn't watching the races, but again I caught myself. "Have you ever seen a race before?"

"Only on TV."

We sat quietly for a few minutes. I had no idea what to say now. She was with me when she was supposed to be with Sirocco or at least watching the rest of the first race. I had been a total jerk the last time I saw her, and I hadn't started off very well today, either, but she was still here. I didn't get it.

"So other than your dad not having a job, how are things going?"

I looked out at the parking lot. "What do you want to do?"

"I thought we were drinking—"

"I mean for a career."

She drew her eyebrows down. "Why?"

"My friend says the reason I blabbed so much to you at the lodge is because I should be seeing a shrink."

Angela smiled. "I haven't thought about being a psychologist."

"So why do I keep unloading on you?"

Looking down at her tea, she said softly, "Probably for the same reason I keep coming back to see you."

I wasn't sure I had heard her correctly until she took a bashful peek at me over her mug. When she saw me looking at her, she turned bright red. Even her forehead, which I could still see a little when she looked back down, was red.

I had to clear my throat before I could speak. "Why is that?"

She shrugged and shifted on her chair. "Do you believe in fate?"

"I don't know."

She laughed lightly. "I think, for fate, or for whatever reason, we're . . . we're drawn to each other."

The only consolation I had at the moment was that she was obviously as uncomfortable as I was.

"What's your last name?"

"Hesse."

"My name is—"

"Sandro Birch," she finished with me. Her blush, which had only begun to fade, came back full force.

"How'd you know?"

"When Phil and Alan were talking about the team at the party, they talked about you."

I was diverted. "What did they say?"

"Alan was giving Phil a hard time, saying that you were going to be able to beat him this season."

"How'd you know it was me?"

"There aren't that many Sandros in this world. In fact, I think you pointed that out to me before."

"You came up here to see me," I realized. She blushed again, and this time I felt my face flush, too. "Why?"

She spread her hands out in front of her on the table. "I told you—"

"Fate?"

"Yeah."

"Just from meeting me once."

"Twice," she said softly.

"Look, I gotta get back," I said suddenly.

"What's wrong?"

"I think I'm supposed to be with the team or something."

"Sandro, I'm not stalking you or anything. I just wanted to get to know you a little better, to see if—"

"If what?"

"Never mind," she said. "You're right. This is stupid. I shouldn't be here, and you need to get back to the team." She stood up. "Let's go."

"Angela—" But I was talking to her back. Quickly, I got up and half-jogged to catch up with her. As I got to her side, our hands brushed. She jerked away.

"Look, I'm not saying I'm not interested—"

"You don't have to say it," she interrupted. "I understand just fine."

"No, I don't think you do. I—"

She was walking awfully fast, so I reached out and grabbed her arm. "Angela."

It took a second before she looked at me, and when she did, I saw tears welling in her eyes. I took a deep breath. "I—" I didn't know where to begin.

"It's okay, Sandro." She gave me a sad smile. "You're not

the first person to think I'm really flaky. Half my family can't even understand me. I don't need you to tell me I'm flipping you out. I can read the signs just fine."

She turned and walked away.

"It's fate," I blurted out.

Spinning around, and looking a little shocked, she said, "What?"

"It's fate," I repeated. "That's what my problem is with this whole thing."

"I don't understand."

"I don't believe in fate," I said. "Or rather, I believe fate is crap."

Her face clouded over. "Oh. I see."

"But I'd really like it if you'd stick around for my next race. I could use some support."

She stared for a moment. "I came up to watch the ski races," she said.

"So you'll stay?"

"Yeah."

When we got to the lodge, I opened the door for her, and she smiled. With that smile, I thought maybe I hadn't screwed everything up too badly.

I was so wrapped up in that thought that I didn't see Sirocco until he was less than six inches from my face. "Tell me you didn't walk on my turf."

I went to step around him, and he stepped with me, so I put my hands up on his shoulders and moved him away from me. He shoved me, hard, and slammed me back into the door.

Before I could move, Mr. Risty was between us.

"That's enough!" he thundered. "Or you're both off the team!"

For a second, I wasn't sure Sirocco had heard. Was he going to take my head off anyway? Before he could move, Angela stepped in.

"Is this about me?" she asked in a very sweet voice.

"Yeah," Sirocco said.

"Did you just call me 'turf'?"

"Well, I—"

"Your *turf*?" Her voice went up a little. "You think I'm a carpet of grass for you to walk on?"

"Babe, I—"

"I'm not your *babe*, I'm not your *turf*, I'm not your *anything*!" And she left.

I would have followed her, but Risty was still standing right in front of me. He was trying hard not to smile. Looking at Sirocco's shocked expression, I didn't even try.

"Well, ahem," Risty cleared his throat. "Now that we've had that lesson on political correctness, I'd like both of you to join the rest of our team downstairs."

I hesitated. I really wanted to go find Angela. I took a step forward, and Sirocco glared at me.

"Now, gentlemen, or I will withdraw both of you from the second run."

"We'd lose the competition," Sirocco said.

"And?" Risty crossed his arms over his chest.

Scowling, Sirocco turned and headed for the stairs. I looked in the direction that Angela had gone. I couldn't see her anywhere.

"Sandro?"

Sighing, I scanned the tables one more time before following Sirocco downstairs.

- - -

Apparently the rumors of the poker game had made it to the coaches' ears, although they hadn't been able to confirm it. That, combined with overall slow times and the near-fight between Sirocco and me, had Risty in a foul mood. After going over results and discussing the next race, he passed judgment.

"After we're done scouting, everyone goes directly to the Chalet at the top. You will all wait there, as a team, until it is your turn to race." A lot of us groaned, but he chose to stare at me. "If you are not at the Chalet when I get up there, I will pull you from the second race and suspend you from the next competition as well. Do I make myself clear?"

"Yes, Coach!" we all mumbled, shouted, or groaned.

I took my time getting to my skis and getting in the lift line. Sirocco and the other guys had already gone up, which was fine by me. I was hoping Angela would see me and come out to talk, but she didn't.

We'd be racing in reverse, from slowest to fastest. I would be tenth from last. That would have been plenty of time to talk to Angela, but I was stuck up at the Chalet. At least when I was done I wouldn't have to wait very long to know the overall standings.

It always amazed me how different slalom runs could be, not just from day to day, but from hour to hour, too. We were given the pattern of the course, but no one was allowed to ski it until the race itself. That eliminated the "home mountain" advantage.

The snow was usually the best in the morning, but not all of us could make two runs before lunch. In the afternoon, the sun had had time to work on the snow, melting it in places, making it sticky and slow. But the shadows from the trees moved, too, and sometimes when the snow was in the shadows again, it froze in a solid sheet.

When I entered the Chalet, I wasn't surprised to see that Sirocco's table was full. He gave me a glare as I walked by, and Tangley gave me a quick grin, but otherwise, I was ignored. I found a table of Vail skiers, asked if I could have one of their chairs, and then I pulled it over to the window. I would probably ski better if I weren't distracted, anyway.

Because so many skiers had disqualified in the first run, there were approximately sixty skiers before me. Each race would take a minimum of two minutes. When you added time between skiers, and the fact that some of the first skiers would take almost three minutes to make the run, then it became more like four minutes per skier. Which gave me about four hours to think.

Between Alessandro, Sirocco, and Angela, I had a lot to think about.

When my name was called for the fifteen-minute warning, I immediately got up and went outside. I was tired of being cooped up in the Chalet. Even if all I could do was stand around on my skis, at least I was moving. And now that Sirocco, Tangley, and I were the last members of our team still at the top, things were even more uncomfortable.

The afternoon sun wasn't very strong, and a good wind

had picked up, making it chilly. I kept stretching and moving around, doing various exercises to keep warm. I desperately wanted a cigarette.

The skier before me got in the starting gate. As I listened to his countdown, my stomach tightened up. Why was I getting nervous about someone else's race?

Mr. Eliot, one of our assistants, came over. "You're up next."

I nodded, afraid that if I opened my mouth I might throw up on him.

"The time you need to beat is—"

I shook my head vehemently. "Don't tell me."

"But if you know what you're aiming for—"

I shook my head again.

He sighed. "Okay. Can I tell you how everyone else has looked on the course?"

Once more, I shook my head.

"Okay. Good luck." And he turned and walked away.

I moved over to the starting gate, waiting for Mrs. Webster to give me a nod. At least I hadn't thrown up again. Mrs. Webster nodded, and I slid into the gate. With the starting wand resting lightly against the top of my ski boot, I studied the beginning of the course. The countdown started, and I began rocking, looking for the rhythm that would launch me out of the booth at the exact second I had my best momentum.

I had a fast start, but almost immediately hit a sheet of ice. I hadn't expected the top to be icy already. Maybe I should have listened to Eliot.

Then I was in the gates, cutting hard into the mountain,

shifting my weight as quickly and precisely as I could. Coming off a wide turn that led into the midstretch of the course, I caught an edge and nearly wiped out. I held it together, barely, and cut the next gate so close I almost wrapped my ski around it. The next two gates were hard, but then I was back in control.

As I entered the final stretch, I could tell the base of the mountain was much warmer than the top. The snow was sticking to my skis, grabbing them, and trying to bog them down. I was going to have to start waxing my skis between runs.

Crossing the finish line, I heard a lot of cheers. It took a second or two to pull to a stop and take my goggles off. I looked up at my time; it was good, but I had no idea how the other skiers had done. Risty was jumping up and down.

As soon as I had my skis off, I walked over to him.

"Excellent, Sandro! Really excellent! That was the fastest run on this course by almost a second and a half."

"How am I standing overall?"

"You're in first, by over two seconds."

That meant Sirocco would only have to match my time to beat me. And the other eight skiers—including Tangley—still had a chance to beat me, too.

Compared to the wait at the top of the mountain, this was going to be torture.

I moved over to where the spectators were.

"Wow, Sandro, that was amazing!"

I turned to find Angela standing next to me. She put her arm around my waist and gave me half a hug.

"I mean, everyone else looked fast but you were—"

"My boy!" Alessandro boomed from behind Angela. "That's my son who skis like a champion! No way is anyone going to beat that time!"

I tried to ignore the looks everyone else was giving us. "Someone could beat that time," I said. "And nine others beat me in the first run."

"You were perfect," Alessandro continued. "Great form, good line, nice turns—"

"You have no idea what you're talking about," I said shortly. "Back off."

He looked hurt. "I came to watch your first race," he said.

"You missed it. The race started at nine–thirty."

He tried again. "I'm here to give you support."

"You're here because you don't have anything to do. Why don't you give Mom some real support and get a job?"

"I'm looking for a job, but—"

"Looking real hard when you sleep in past ten each morning," I muttered.

A cheer went up from the rest of the spectators, and I turned to watch as Tangley came down the bottom of the run. The part of his race that we got to see was clean, but his time was almost three full seconds slower than mine. My combined time was faster than his.

"He must have had a serious problem somewhere at the top," I said to Angela.

She smiled at me.

"You out-skied him, just like you out-ski everyone else!" Alessandro said loudly.

"Would you stop it? Or better yet, just leave."

"I'm here—"

"And I wish you weren't."

"Your mom wants you to give me a chance."

"I've given you several. You sit around the house, waiting for chances."

"Sandro—" Angela put her hand on my arm.

Ignoring her, I continued, "You're just using her again, and she's too blind to see it. What are you doing, waiting till the bank account's empty before you leave?"

"I'm not leaving your mother. But I'm thinking I'd like to leave you."

"So leave!"

"Actually, that sounds like a great idea," Angela said loudly.

"What?"

"I'm leaving now. I just wanted to say good-bye."

"But—" I sputtered.

"Maybe I'll see you around," she said.

"I don't have your number!"

She just shook her head and walked away.

"Wait!" I tried to follow her, but Alessandro stepped in front of me.

"You've got a real attitude problem. Where does all this anger come from? You need to come to Italy, learn peace and relaxation."

I shoved past him, looking for Angela, but she had disappeared into the crowd. There were three parking lots and a shuttle that went to two more. I had no idea which direction she had gone.

"You've got to quit blaming everyone else for your problems, Sandrino."

"My name is Sandro!" I yelled at him. "And I don't blame *everyone* else for my problems, I blame *you*!"

The crowd all around us was silent and staring, but then they turned and began cheering. The last Vail skier was coming down the slope.

Even as he came off the ridge, I could tell he wasn't going as fast as Tangley had. He wasn't tucking nearly enough, and his skis were all over the place. It was like he couldn't decide on a line to follow.

"You're still in front." Alessandro tried to put his arm around my shoulder.

I shrugged him off and walked away from him. I scanned the crowd again. Angela had said she wanted to watch a race; surely, she wouldn't leave this close to the end. She had to be here, still watching. I walked through the tables, toward the closest parking lot, thinking that maybe she had stopped there to see the last skiers before leaving. She wasn't anywhere.

"She left," Alessandro said. I hadn't realized he had been following me.

"I wish you would, too."

"You don't believe people. She said she was leaving, but you don't believe her. I say I'm not leaving, and you—"

"Shut up! Get out of my face! I don't need you trying to psychoanalyze me!"

"And then there's all that anger—"

All that anger almost exploded on his face. I just barely stopped myself from decking him right there.

I turned to walk away from him, and I could feel him right behind me. I spun around, and he almost ran into me. "What are you doing?"

"I want to be with you when you win your first race," he said. Every time he talked about my races, he was loud and had a big grin on his face. I suddenly realized what was going on.

"*If* I win, it's *my* race and *I* won it. You didn't do a damn thing."

A gasp went up from the crowd, and for a split second, I thought they were all listening to my personal soap opera. Then I looked up at the course just in time to see Sirocco trying to get his skis back underneath him. He got them together, and I really thought he had it under control as he went into the next gate. But he must have overcorrected, and he swung way too far around it. He had no chance to make the next gate.

As he disappeared in a puff of snow by the trees, I suddenly realized what had just happened.

"You won!" Alessandro said, clapping me on the back. "A regular chip off the old block!" He started to pull me forward. "Let's go! Don't they do award ceremonies or something for you?"

"I'd like to make sure my teammate's okay," I said, still watching the slope. Sirocco might be a jerk, but that didn't mean I wanted him hurt or out for the season. A couple of seconds later, I saw Sirocco skiing down on the outside edge of the slope. He appeared to be okay.

"Come on," Alessandro said again. Then, louder, "Where does the winner go?"

I jerked my arm away from him. "Stop! You're making me look like a poor sport," I hissed.

"Poor sports are losers—"

"Poor sports are winners who are jerks," I said. I had seen enough of them to know I didn't want to become one.

A lady tapped me on the shoulder. "I think they want all team members over by the flag," she said.

"Thanks," I said, smiling. I thought I'd finally get away from Alessandro. I was disgusted when he followed me again.

Sirocco was just stepping out of his bindings when I walked by.

"Tough luck," I said sympathetically.

"Bite me."

"I mean it—"

"Bite me," he said again, and then he picked up his skis. "Pieces of junk," he muttered and dropped them in the trash can.

I felt my jaw drop, and for the life of me I didn't think I could shut it again. He had just thrown away equipment worth hundreds of dollars. My fingers were itching to yank the skis out. I had pride, but I had even more common sense.

Just then, Eliot walked up, shaking his head. "Poor sportsmanship, Phil. That can cost you a starting position next meet."

Sirocco scowled at him.

"I mean it, Phil. Pull 'em out. You had a lousy race. Don't act like it's your equipment's fault."

As Sirocco lifted the skis out of the trash, Eliot glanced over at me. "Get to the flag pole, Sandro."

I nodded and began walking again. I could feel my unwanted shadow next to me.

"Excuse me, sir?" Eliot reached out.

"Yes?"

"It's a team meeting."

"I know," Alessandro said, smiling broadly. "I'm going with my son."

Eliot blinked. "I didn't . . . I'm sorry, Mr. Birch—"

"Scarpettarini. Alessandro Scarpettarini."

"Okay, but we ask that parents and spectators wait over there," he pointed to the lodge. "We'll be done in a moment."

"But—"

"It gets too crowded with everyone. Team members only."

"Sandro! Son! I'll meet you—"

"Go home!" I shouted without looking back at him. "Just go!"

11

Unfortunately, Alessandro would not leave. I had to listen to his cheers and loud comments to the crowd in general for almost five minutes.

The results and ribbon ceremony weren't as hyped as the Olympics, but it was certainly the most embarrassing thing I had ever been through. As soon as they handed me my blue ribbon, I turned to walk away, only to be told I had to actually climb on the platform with Tangley and the Vail skier.

When I finally broke away, I headed for the team locker room. I had to go get my boots off and grab my bag.

"Sandrino! Sandrino!"

Not only didn't Alessandro get a hint; he still couldn't get my name right.

"Sandro!"

I turned around. "What?"

"Come on, let's go celebrate your victory!"

Rolling my eyes, I continued walking into the lodge.

He caught up with me. "The Jeep's out in Lot Two. We'll go get your mom—"

"She's working—"

"She can leave early tonight," he said confidently. "We'll all go out to dinner together—"

"I'm riding the bus back to school, and then I'm going home."

"But—"

"Will you just leave?" I asked. "Just leave me alone!"

"Something wrong, Sandro?" Mr. Risty asked. "Is he bothering you?"

"Yes," I said at the same time Alessandro said, "No."

"I just want him to ride home with me," Alessandro added.

"I'm afraid I can't allow that," Mr. Risty said.

"I'm his father," Alessandro bristled. "Alessandro Scarpettarini."

"The only parent that signed his permission slip and medical release is Ms. *Birch*," Mr. Risty said. "And without a note from her, Sandro has to ride the bus home. It's school policy." He glanced at me. "Hurry up, Sandro. Bus leaves in five."

I disappeared into the team room, and when I came back, Alessandro was gone.

After I got my skis and poles loaded on the bus, I found an empty seat and sat down, adjusting my Discman for the long ride home. Sirocco and company only thought they were rejecting me. I was rejecting them.

When we pulled into the school parking lot, I was relieved to see that Mom's Jeep wasn't there. Shouldering my skis, I started to walk to the east bus stop, then changed my mind. I headed to the west one, the one that would take me into town.

- - -

"Sandro!"

"Hey! How'd you do?"

"Look, it's the big man!"

I had to grin. Walking into the ski shop was better than anything else I could have done.

After shaking hands with LeMoyne and Kolton, I said, "I'm officially a ski god."

"You beat Sirocco!" LeMoyne exclaimed. "Awesome! I wish I could have been there to see him get creamed!"

"I only beat him in the second run," I began.

"Then you must have blown him off the mountain, to catch and pass his time," Kolton observed.

"He fell, actually, so he pretty much gave the race to me."

LeMoyne whooped. He was practically dancing. "I can't believe I missed it!"

Jade wandered over. "Missed what?"

"Sandro beat Sirocco," LeMoyne said.

Jade turned to me, but before she could say anything, Kolton interrupted. "Those of you on the clock need to get everything cleaned up so we can all get out of here."

LeMoyne immediately headed for the skis, and Jade put her hand on my arm. "You're coming with me tonight," she purred before gliding over to the boots.

Kolton raised his eyebrows at me. "She knows you're gonna be the ticket tonight."

I grinned before wandering over to help LeMoyne. The

faster the shop closed, the faster we could all get out of here and go party.

- - -

Before, I had always thought that all the rich kids were in the same group. After hanging out with Sirocco and his friends for the last couple of weeks, I had learned they had their own subdivisions. It was refreshing to find new people to talk to. With the exception of Webster, everyone else seemed to be in awe of Sirocco, and all conversations revolved around him. I was looking forward to something different.

Unfortunately, between Jade and LeMoyne, I ended up talking about Sirocco and his races almost as much as I would have if I had been with him. After a few hours, I was able to get away from most of the crowd, but Jade and LeMoyne stayed with me.

"How were things today?"

"Easy," Jade said.

"For a Friday afternoon," LeMoyne agreed.

"Anyone interesting come in?"

"Nah," LeMoyne said.

"You looking for a girl?" Jade asked.

"When I've got you? You're kidding, right?" I asked, putting my arm around her. I was joking, and totally caught off guard when she leaned back against my shoulder and put her hand on my thigh.

"Good answer," she said.

LeMoyne tried unsuccessfully to cover a laugh with a cough. "Well, it's time for me to get going. I'll catch you at practice tomorrow morning," he said, nodding toward me.

I wanted desperately to jump up and follow him. I

didn't want Jade hanging on me. But I didn't want to go home yet, either.

"So," she said, moving her hand a little higher on my thigh. "What else can you do?"

Turn bright red, I thought about saying. My face was on fire. It was a struggle to talk without clearing my throat first, but I managed. "What do you mean?"

"All I know is that you ski," she said, "and that you work when you're not skiing."

"Yeah."

"So what else do you do? Do you go to movies?"

"Not really."

"Why not?"

"Waste of money," I said. "It'll be on TV sooner or later for free."

"Yeah, but it's not as good on TV."

"It's not bad, either."

She sat up and away from me a little. "So you just like to save money. Would you go see a movie if it was free?"

"Of course."

"Good. Then we'll go see one tomorrow night," she said, leaning into me again. "I'm buying."

"No."

"Excuse me?" She almost jumped away from me this time.

"Thank you," I said, trying to soften my tone. "Thank you for the thought, but I don't need charity."

"It's not charity," she said stiffly.

"You just said you'd pay."

"And you'd pay me back later," she said, her eyes

smoky. She reached up and rubbed her hand on the top of my head. "You'd look better with hair, but I like the way the fuzz feels."

"Jade—"

"Sandro, I don't usually have to do the asking."

"I'm sure you don't."

"My point is that I like you."

"I kind of got that."

She sighed. "Don't you like me?"

I stood up. "I think you're pretty cool."

"You think LeMoyne's pretty cool."

"Yeah."

"So I'm like a friend."

Actually, I wasn't even sure I'd go that far. She was a girl I worked with, someone who I could go to parties with. Just the two of us together, even at a party like this, wasn't very comfortable. "Yeah, you're like a friend."

"Don't you want a girlfriend?"

"No."

Her eyebrows went up. "Do you want a boyfriend?"

I glared at her. "I don't want anyone."

"Why not?"

There wasn't a point in answering her. She didn't really want to know about me; she just wanted to know why I wasn't in awe of her. "Jade, you're beautiful, and usually you're pretty smart." I ducked as she tossed a throw pillow at me. "I don't want to wreck our friendship," I said, trying to sound sincere. "And I definitely don't want to make it awkward at work."

"Okay," she said, shrugging.

"Want to go play quarters?"

She sighed and rolled her eyes before she looked at the quarters table. "Why not?"

I grabbed her hand and pulled her up off the couch. "Let's go."

Moving to the table started off as a good idea. Jade was smiling again, and I was able to bum a cigarette from somebody. But Jade began doing shots, lots of them. And I was tired. The ski meet felt like it had been weeks ago, but it had only been this morning. It was time to go home.

"Come on, Jade. I'll walk you home."

"I'm not ready to go," she said, pouting.

"Time to go."

"I'll walk her home," said the burly blond guy sitting next to her.

"Really?" Jade turned big eyes to him.

He smiled what was probably a charming smile. It looked like a tiger watching a baby antelope to me. He had been eyeing her since the moment we sat down. I guessed he was in his twenties, and he was pretty toasted. On top of that, he wasn't a local.

"Let's go, Jade," I said, putting my hands on the back of her chair.

She leaned her head back to look up at me. "But I don't want to go," she repeated.

"But we've got to go," I said, matching her whine.

"Dude, she don't have to go if she don't want to," the blond guy said.

"Yeah," she said. "He can walk me home."

I knelt down and dropped my voice. "Do you know this guy?"

"Yeah!"

"What's his name?"

Not missing a beat, she turned and asked, "Hey, what's your name?"

"Kyle," he said, smirking at me.

"His name's Kyle, and he said he'd walk me home," she said airily.

"Jade," I said firmly. When she didn't look at me, I said her name again, and waited until I had her full attention. "Jade, you came here with me, and I have to make sure you get home safely. I don't want anybody to hurt you."

"Hey!" Kyle said.

I ignored him. "You're drunk. I don't want to leave and then have you do something you might regret later." *And blame me for*, but I didn't say that. Even if she didn't blame me, I would.

We stared into each other's eyes for a few seconds. "Think about my mother," I said softly.

Then she sighed. "Okay. Okay."

I stood up and started to pull her chair back.

"You don't have to listen to him," Kyle said. "You can stay here with us."

She stood up. "I came with Sandro," she said. "I should go home with him."

I didn't like the way that sounded, but since she was going to let me walk her home, I didn't say anything.

"I'd be better to go home with."

She laughed, back in her flirtatious mode. "Give me your phone number, and we can talk about it some other time."

"I'll only be here for another week," he said, reaching for a pen.

"Don't bother," I said, holding Jade's jacket.

"Excuse me?" Kyle said.

"Don't bother giving her your phone number. She's not just a spring fling."

Jade was looking up at me with a strange expression. Kyle was glaring at me. "She just said she wanted my number!"

"Not anymore."

"I don't like the way you try to make her do things," he said, standing up. I thought he had looked big sitting down, but that was nothing compared to what happened when he stood up. "I think she should be able to make her own choice."

"She can—" I began.

Grabbing my arm, Jade said, "Sandro's right. I'm not a spring fling. Let's go home."

We walked out into the quiet street. Jade still had hold of my arm. She was holding on pretty tight. After we had walked about a block, she whispered, "Thank you."

"Sure."

"No one's ever said anything like that about me."

I was confused. "Like what?"

"Not being just a fling."

"You deserve better than that."

She squeezed my arm even harder. "But not you."

I laughed. "You deserve much better than me."

"What's wrong, Sandro? Really. Why do you keep everyone away?"

I was startled. I thought she was just a flighty, selfish girl. I hadn't realized she actually paid attention to people around her, especially me.

"Love sucks."

"You've been in love?"

"No."

"You shouldn't judge things without trying them. Haven't you ever read *Green Eggs and Ham?*" she asked.

"Some things you don't have to experience to know they're bad."

"You don't ever want to be in love?"

"No."

"Why not?"

"It serves no purpose."

Jade wrinkled her nose at me. "You wouldn't be here if it weren't for love."

"You're right," I said easily. "But love complicates things too much. It takes too much from you."

"It gives you more than it takes," she argued.

"How often have you been in love?"

"Enough."

I could tell she would stay here all night talking to me, talking about love. I was ready to go home. Pulling her roughly into a hug, I kissed her. It wasn't a long kiss, and it really didn't do anything for me, but it shut her up.

When she stepped back from me, I tapped the tip of her nose with my finger. "Now go inside, go to sleep, and we'll see if you remember any of this in the morning."

"I'll remember," she promised. "And I'll get you to believe in love before we're done."

I watched her walk up to the front door and fumble for her keys. Then she let herself in without looking back at me.

I started my walk home. I put my hands in my coat pocket, and my fingers encountered a piece of paper. I pulled it out, but I didn't recognize it, and there wasn't enough light to read what was on it. I shoved it back in my pocket. Although I thought about what Jade had said, it was Angela I kept seeing in my mind. So I was in a pretty good mood—until I saw that the lights in our apartment were still on.

Cursing, I decided I'd just sit on the stairs and have a smoke. Then I remembered that I didn't have any cigarettes. It was too cold to stay outside for long, but I sat on the steps till my buns were numb. The light was still on when I finally went up.

The front door swung open as I reached for the door-knob. Mom was glaring at me.

"Hi! How was work?" I asked.

"Don't give me that!" she snapped in a low tone. "Where the hell have you been?"

"At a—"

"Shh!" she interrupted, pointing to the couch. Alessandro was sprawled out, snoring.

"I was at a party," I said in a quieter voice.

"Why didn't you come home? You told him you'd come home."

"I did not!"

"Shh!"

"I didn't," I repeated. "I told *him* to go home. I never said *I* was coming."

"Sandro," she warned.

"It's the truth."

"He wanted to take you out to dinner to celebrate! He wanted to have an evening together in your honor."

I was shaking my head.

"Sandro, he was so proud of you! He could hardly speak a straight sentence when he came to get me from work. And then you didn't come home. You didn't even call."

"Sorry," I said sarcastically. "I've never had to call home to Daddy before."

"He's been here for three weeks now, and you still act like—"

"Like he's a bum who can't get a job? Like he's a player who can't make a commitment?"

She glared at me in such a way that I almost thought she was going to slap me. "Your judgment—"

"—is just fine. It's *your* judgment that needs an adjustment."

"What?"

"How can you be so hopelessly stupid?" I demanded. "How can you really believe—"

"How can *you* be so cynical and arrogant? I thought I raised you better than that."

"You raised me, and you kept waiting for a fantasy that never—"

"He's on the couch, Sandro! He's here, and he's a part of our lives now, whether you like it or not."

"Well, I don't!"

She just stared at me for a long moment. Then she crossed her arms over her chest and said, "Go to your room."

I laughed. I really couldn't help it.

"I'm serious. Go to your room."

Even though that was exactly what I had wanted to do, I shook my head. "I think I'll get something to eat first."

"Dinner was hours ago. You weren't here, so you missed out. Go to your room."

"I'm not ten, Mom. You can't send me to my room."

"I can when you're behaving like a child."

"I'll stop acting like a child the minute after you do."

She bit her lip. Tears were glistening in her eyes. "Believing in love doesn't make me a child," she said. "But not giving someone a chance does make you a jerk."

"I'll just get something to eat," I said quietly. "Then I'll go to my room like a good little boy."

I took two steps to the kitchen, and then stopped short. Propped up in the corner were a black and purple pair of short, side-cut slalom skis and matching poles. They were even a better brand than Sirocco's. My mouth went dry.

"He got them for you," Mom said quietly. "He said your equipment was too outdated for your talent."

"He bought them for me? He paid for them?"

"We bought them."

"You mean you did."

"It was his idea and—"

"And your money, more than you can afford." I turned to the refrigerator, although I was itching to touch the skis. "Take them back."

"We can afford them now."

"How? You're feeding one more person on the same salary." I opened the fridge and surveyed the assortment of take-out boxes. "And he's got more expensive tastes as it is."

"He'll get some interviews lined up soon and—"

"Hard to get interviews when he doesn't even apply," I muttered.

"Can't you accept his gift for what it is?"

"I do. It's an attempt to bribe me, and he didn't even pay for it." I took a soda and the rest of a block of cheese from the fridge. Then I grabbed some crackers and a knife. "I'm going to my room now, Mom." I paused and glanced at the skis. "And I'd rather not see those again."

"Why not?" Alessandro asked from the couch. Without answering him, I turned and walked away.

As I shut my bedroom door, I found myself wishing for a lock. I was afraid that one of them would come in and want to talk some more. I was sick of talking, when all we did was go in endless circles. And I was afraid I would end up accepting the skis.

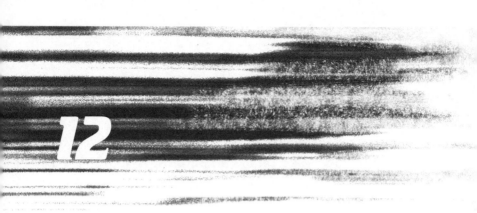

12

LeMoyne and I met at the corner and walked to school together. Saturdays were early calisthenics, because the ski areas didn't want us using space and lifts that their tourists had paid for. And because so many of us worked, the team had talked Mr. Risty into 6 A.M. weekend practice times. As we walked over, LeMoyne and I wondered why we had ever thought that was a good idea.

"So how was Jade last night?"

"Drunk."

"Well, yeah, but how was she?" he asked, jabbing me with his elbow and winking.

I shook my head. "It wasn't like that."

"It sure looked like that."

"Looks can be deceiving."

"You know she wants you."

"Whatever."

It was weird approaching the deserted school in darkness. There were only three cars in the lot, all parked close to the gym doors. That's where we went, and stepped inside, temporarily blinded by the glaring lights.

Risty smiled when he saw us and made a note on his clipboard. "Workout's on the board, guys. Soon as you're done, you're done, okay?"

We nodded and shed our jackets, then checked the whiteboard. We had to do two hundred sit-ups and push-ups in sets of twenty, perform a variety of weight exercises, and run twenty laps of the gym.

"We'd better get started," LeMoyne said, "or we'll be late for work."

"Right." The shop opened at seven thirty, but we weren't scheduled to be there until eight. "What do you want to do first?"

"Let's get the weights done first," he said. "We can always run or do the sit-ups at home if we need to."

I grinned. "Good plan. We won't be late for work." I looked around. "I thought these practices were mandatory."

"So did I," he said, looking at the other four people in the gym. "And I hope Risty considers attendance when he decides who gets to race."

We had just finished all of the weight work when Sirocco and Webster showed up.

"Let's run next," I said. "I'd rather run inside than in the snow."

He nodded, and we started circling the gym at an easy jog. Webster and Sirocco fell in behind us.

"You and Jade really didn't tango?" LeMoyne asked me.

"From what I hear, he won't tango with anyone," Sirocco

said to Webster, but making sure he was loud enough for us to hear.

LeMoyne looked over his shoulder but I just shook my head and kept jogging.

"At first, I thought it was just the local chicks he wasn't interested in, but Angela says—"

I turned around, and Sirocco just managed to skid to a stop before plowing into me. Webster had slower reflexes, and he and LeMoyne collided and went down in a tumble. We ignored them.

"Don't talk about Angela."

"Why not?"

"You're not good enough for her," I said, knowing it was lame. The whole thing was lame, but I couldn't seem to help it. Just thinking about him and Angela together could make me see red.

"I'm better than good enough."

LeMoyne was pulling on my shoulder, and Webster was flanking Sirocco.

"You suck," was all I could grind out.

Sirocco was so close I could see the gray flecks in his blue eyes. "Say that again, and it'll be the last thing you say."

"Come on, Phil." Webster tried to get between us.

"Gentlemen!" Risty's voice whipped across the gym. "Front and center, now!"

Neither of us was willing to back down. Webster and LeMoyne had to pull us apart and lead us over to where Risty was waiting.

"What's the problem?"

"No problem," Sirocco said.

"This is twice in two days, Phil. I think there's a problem." Risty looked at me. I kept my mouth shut. He sighed and shook his head. "Okay, then, here's the deal. The two of you run together. You stay together for each lap, and you keep running until you're ready to talk. Go."

"But—" Sirocco started.

"Go. Start running now, because for every second you delay, you owe me one lunch detention."

Sirocco didn't seem to understand. "But—"

"That's one."

"Come on, Risty—" he tried again.

"Two."

I turned to start jogging.

"You have to start together," Mr. Risty said. "And you're now at four days detention."

I glared at Sirocco. He crossed his arms over his chest.

"Don't feel like cooperating, Phil?"

"I'm not going to run with him," Sirocco said. "And I'm not doing detention either."

Risty's face turned red. "Then—"

"All right, all right, I'll run."

"Too late. Go home. And don't come to practice till you bring your parents in with you."

"I said I'd—"

"Go home," Risty turned back to his clipboard.

Sirocco stared at the top of Risty's head. "Let's go, Alan."

Without looking up from his clipboard, Risty said,

"Anyone cutting out of practice early is out of the next meet."

I was tired of the drama. "Come on, LeMoyne," I said, tapping him on the shoulder. We started our laps. Webster fell in step with us.

We ran in silence for so long that I thought we'd be able to finish all twenty laps without saying anything at all. No such luck.

"He's really not that bad," Webster said.

LeMoyne snorted. "You can't be serious."

"He's just used to getting his way."

"So he's spoiled," I said.

Webster grinned. "Somethin' like that."

We completed another lap, and I tried to get my question straight. "Uh, did Phil talk to Angela last night?"

LeMoyne glanced at me.

"Yeah. We went to a party in Golden. She was there."

"Oh." My mind was spinning.

After hesitating, Webster added, "She wasn't very nice to him, though."

"Oh?"

"Then why'd Sirocco say he talked to her?" LeMoyne asked.

"He wanted to get to Sandro."

I grunted. LeMoyne laughed.

"He's pissed," Webster said seriously. "Be careful."

"That jerk-off can't hurt Sandro," LeMoyne scoffed.

Webster looked at me, but didn't say anything. We finished our last lap.

"Time to go to work," LeMoyne said.

I held my hand out to Webster. "Thanks, man."

We shook hands, and then he headed to the weights. LeMoyne and I promised Risty we'd do the rest of our calisthenics at home, and he shortened my sentence to two days of detention. Then LeMoyne and I headed for the shop.

- - -

Work was refreshingly normal. For those few hours, I could almost forget everything. For those few hours, the ski team and my newfound father didn't exist.

I had been worried about Jade, but she took everything in stride. She acted like it was all fine, and I was too afraid to ask if she remembered everything. Before I knew it, we were closing up.

"Hey, who's got the party tonight?" Robert asked.

"Not me," I said.

"No cash?" LeMoyne guessed.

"No cash."

"I don't want to go party alone," Robert said. "How about I pick up a couple six-packs, and we go hang out at my place?"

LeMoyne glanced at me. Robert was cool, but he didn't exactly fit in. He had taken a semester off from college to ski, and had somehow never gone back. I didn't know how old he was, and outside of the ski shop staff, I wasn't sure he had any friends.

"Come on, I'll buy," Robert pressed.

I nodded. It would beat going home.

"Sure," LeMoyne said, shrugging. "Sandro and I will pick up a movie and meet you there."

"Jade? Kolton? Want to come?"

"I'll see what Torey says. Maybe we'll come by for a bit."

"No thanks, Robert," Jade said.

"Why? You got other plans?"

"Maybe."

"And they're too good to share with us?"

"Not exactly," she said, glancing sideways at me.

Robert looked at me, and then at her, and his eyebrows went up.

"I'll see you guys tomorrow," Jade said, grabbing her jacket and heading out the door.

"Bet she forgot to clock out," Kolton grumbled.

"I'll sign her out," I said.

"I'll do it," he said. "I just wish she would remember once in a while."

LeMoyne and I took a while trying to decide which movie to rent. I hated video stores. Rows and rows and rows of choices. Too many choices.

"This one?" I asked, holding up a new release.

"Seen it. This one?" he asked.

"Looks dumb. How about this?"

"Chick flick."

Sighing, I stuck my hands in my jacket pockets, and discovered the paper again. I had meant to look at it that night after the party and simply forgot. Now I pulled it out and stared.

"This one? Sandro? Yo! Sandro, what's that?"

"I don't believe it."

"What?" LeMoyne was peering over my shoulder.

"Angela's number."

"What?" He pulled the paper out of my hand and then whistled. "When did you get it?"

"I didn't." I was trying to think. "She must have slipped it in my pocket."

"You gonna call her?"

I took the paper back from him and put it back in my pocket. "Not right now. Let's get a movie and get out of here."

Somehow I managed to tune out all of his wise cracks on the walk over to Robert's house. Kolton and Torey dropped by for a little bit, but they didn't stay for the movie. We watched the movie, some action-packed high-budget thing with a minimal plot, and Robert and LeMoyne drank a few beers. The two of them talked about a lot of stuff, but I couldn't have told you what. They didn't seem to notice that I wasn't paying much attention.

As soon as the movie was over, I reached for my jacket.

"You leavin' already?" Robert asked.

"Movie's over."

"Beer's not gone," LeMoyne pointed out.

"We're not supposed to be drinkin' anyway."

"Since when did you get high and mighty?"

"It's part of the athlete's code."

LeMoyne snorted. "Not supposed to smoke, either."

I pulled my jacket on. "You keep my secret, I'll keep yours."

"You're really goin'?"

"Yeah."

"Let me finish this one quick," LeMoyne said.

"Now you're *both* goin'?" Robert almost whined.

"Thanks, Robert," I said by way of an apology. "You workin' tomorrow?"

"Yeah. That's all I do anymore."

LeMoyne stood up and grabbed his coat. "We'll see you tomorrow then."

Robert popped open another beer. "Yep."

As soon as we were out of Robert's building, LeMoyne started laughing. "Man, you are so gone!"

"Who?"

"You!"

"Man, I didn't even have one—"

"I ain't sayin' you're drunk. I'm sayin' you're gone."

"Gone where?"

"In la-la land."

"You're the one who's gone," I said in disgust. "I don't know how many you had, but you're not making any sense."

"You didn't even hear us talkin' about you," LeMoyne laughed.

"What?" My hand was wrapped tightly around the paper in my pocket.

"Robert an' me were talkin' about you, and you didn't even notice!"

"You were not!"

"Were too!"

I stared at LeMoyne for a second then said, "What were you sayin'?"

That set him off again, and I had to wait till he could talk calmly. "You and Jade, mostly."

"Me and Jade what?"

"Whether or not you two are gonna hook up."

"We're not," I said.

"I know that," LeMoyne said. "But it's fun razzin' Robert about it."

"Why?"

"He's got a thing for her."

"Serious?"

"You didn't know?" he asked in surprise.

"Ain't he a little old for her?"

"What do you care? You don't want her." He started laughing again. "That's why you were off in la-la land."

I felt myself flushing. "What do you mean?"

"You were thinkin' about Angela."

"Maybe."

LeMoyne chuckled. "Maybe nothin'. You gonna call her when you get home?"

"Maybe."

"All right. Play it that way." He held his hand out, and we tapped fists. "See ya at work tomorrow."

"Yep." And he turned up his street while I continued on my way.

My walk was over before I knew it, and I was relieved to come home to an empty apartment. In my room, I pulled the paper out and set it on my desk. She had printed her name neatly, without any loops or decorations. And she had included her area code—it would be a long-distance phone call.

I wiped my sweaty palms on my jeans and picked up the phone. Taking a deep breath, I dialed her number before I could think about it again. As the phone rang, I glanced up at the clock. It was past midnight. I slammed the phone down. How had it gotten so late?

My heart was pounding in my ears. I couldn't decide what was worse: that I had called her so late or that I had just hung up the phone like that. I felt like a fool.

What if she had Caller ID? I had only heard about it, and I didn't know exactly what Caller ID showed. Was it just my phone number, or was it my name, too? What would she think of me, calling and hanging up like that? Would she call back?

Five minutes later, my phone was still quiet. I was torn between relief and distress. Maybe she didn't have Caller ID, and she'd never know I called. Or maybe she *did* have Caller ID, and she wasn't going to call me back. There was no way to know without calling her again, and I wasn't about to do that.

I was an idiot to even think about calling her. There was no way she still liked me. And what was all that crap about fate, anyway? The last thing I needed was another female in my life who believed in fairy tales and happy endings.

I picked up the paper and shredded it.

13

"Dude, you're slowin' down!"

LeMoyne didn't answer as he pulled to a stop next to me.

"You're supposed to practice racin'—that means goin' fast, in case you didn't know." I stopped as LeMoyne took a breath—a huge, wheezing, noisy breath. "Oh, come on. You better have that inhaler with you!"

He saved his energy for breathing and just nodded, pulling off a glove and reaching into his jacket pocket. Then he reached into the other one. Then he got a confused look on his face and began going through all his other pockets. His breathing was slowing down, but he was still wheezing pretty badly.

"LeMoyne?"

"I had . . . it with me. . . . Put it in . . . pocket . . . this morning."

"LeMoyne," I said with alarm, "you're awfully pale for a black dude."

"Think I'll . . . I'll sit for . . . a minute," he said, kind of collapsing on the side of the hill. He sat for a second, then let himself lie down.

"I'm goin' to get ski patrol," I said.

"No. I'll . . . be fine."

"LeMoyne—"

"Sandro—" He wasn't wheezing quite as much.

Uncertain, I stood and waited next to him for a few moments, watching the other skiers go by.

"You know what the problem is?" he said finally.

"You can't seem to remember you're asthmatic," I said flatly.

He grinned. "You're too damn fast on those new skis."

I shifted my skis, covering them in snow. At first, I had considered exchanging them for a different pair, with better colors, but they'd still be the skis Alessandro bought me. Nothing was going to change that. But they had changed my skiing: My turns were tight, my control was perfect, and my times just kept getting faster.

LeMoyne seemed to be breathing much better. He sat up.

"You all right?"

"Yeah. I'll be ready to go in just a sec."

"Good 'nuff."

"You can go on ahead."

"You've got serious oxygen deprivation problems if you think I'd let you ski down by yourself."

"I'll be skiin' by myself anyway," he muttered. "I can't keep up with you even when I *can* breathe! I'll be goin' slow," he added. "*Real slow*."

"So everything's normal," I said. He tried to throw a snowball at me, but missed. I laughed.

We skied down, and he was right; he went really slowly. That was okay. I was able to watch the trees and the people on the lift and the other skiers and the clouds. Maybe going slowly wasn't so bad, every once in a while.

At the base, LeMoyne stepped out of his skis. I looked over at the line for the Super Six.

"Go on, man," LeMoyne said.

"What?" I asked, turning back to look at him.

"Go on. I think I've got another inhaler in my locker at the shop, but I also thought I had one in my pocket. I may be goin' home for one."

"So I should just stay on the bottom run, and you'll meet me down here eventually?"

"I wouldn't do that to you. We'll meet back here in an hour, okay?"

"An hour? It's gonna take you an hour to take a puff?"

"I probably should rest for a little while, too," he admitted as he lifted his skis to his shoulder. "An hour?"

"That gonna be enough time?" I asked, half-joking, half-serious. "Don't want you to have any more problems. Maybe you should take the rest of the day off."

"See ya in an hour," he said, crunching away in his boots.

"Later," I said, pushing over toward the lift line.

When I got to the top of the Super Six, I took the cat-walk over to another lift that would take me to the top of the mountain.

As I got to the line, I heard someone holler, "Sandro!"

I figured it was someone from the ski team, so I slid off to the side of the line and let a few people go in front of me.

Looking over my shoulder, I didn't see anyone I recognized at first. Then I realized that Alessandro was standing right in front of me.

"Ready to go?" he said.

"I, uh, I was, someone called me—"

"Yes. I did. Come on. Let's see how good you are." He pushed off to the line. "Come on!"

I didn't want to ride up with him, but I didn't want to go all the way down to the base again, either. I turned to follow him in line.

As we sat on the chair and swung up and away from the ground, he reached in his pocket. "Want one?" he asked.

Without looking, I said, "Sure." I was so used to smoking on the lift that I expected a cigarette. I was startled when I discovered a candy bar instead. I laughed. I couldn't help it.

"It's the best quick energy you can get," he said, taking a bite.

"I prefer cigarettes," I said, trying to hand the candy bar back to him.

"Well, you can't smoke on the lift with me."

I just stared at him for a second. He wouldn't take the candy bar from my hand. The thought of blowing smoke in his face was very appealing. Unfortunately, I had already smoked two of the three cigarettes I was allowing myself these days. I didn't want to go cold turkey, but I knew I needed to cut down. In disgust, I unwrapped the candy and took a vicious bite instead.

"You need to quit smoking."

"I didn't ask for your opinion."

"You don't have to ask. As my son, you get all my opinions for free."

"Then I'll start charging to receive them."

He smiled. "I like your wit. But you should use it for school."

I crushed the wrapper and stuffed it into my pocket.

He pulled a comb out and began pulling it through his hair. I snorted. "What?" he demanded.

"What a waste of time."

"But it's worth it. The ladies almost die for dark, curly hair like ours." He glanced at me as he tucked his comb in his pocket. "You should grow your hair out. It would help you get a girlfriend."

"I don't need your advice on what to do with my hair," I snapped. "And you know nothing about my girlfriend."

"I know you don't have one."

"No, you don't."

"Ah! You have a girlfriend! The one from the meet, perhaps? What is her name?"

"None of your business."

He made a clucking noise with his tongue. "Now you make me think you don't have a girlfriend again."

I refused to look at him.

After a few seconds, he asked, "What are you practicing today?"

"Nothin'."

"You should be practicing every time you put on your skis."

"That sounds dull."

"It is vital to your skiing career. Each time you get on

the lift, you should reflect on the run you just did, and get mentally prepared for the next one. Each run should focus on one aspect. Start with something simple, like your knees. Then, for the whole—"

"Look, I'm not interested in your lecture on Skiing 101."

"But I'm—"

"Giving instructions for a beginner, or maybe an intermediate skier. I'm a little beyond that."

"You're not beyond needing coaching," Alessandro said.

"I didn't say I was beyond *coaching*. I said I was past beginner or intermediate. And my *coaches* agree with me."

"But you don't think I'm good enough to coach you."

I thought it was in my best interest not to answer that.

"The day you think you can beat me—"

"Passed a long time ago," I muttered.

"Your old man isn't that old." When I didn't say anything, he said, "What run are we going to do?"

"You do whatever run you want."

"Are you afraid to ski with me?"

"Psshht." I waved my hand at him.

"It's okay to be afraid."

"I don't believe in wasting my time."

We rode in silence for a few moments. Then, as the end of the lift came into sight, he said, "It would make me very happy to ski just one run with my son."

I groaned. "What is it with you and the sappy crap?"

He just looked at me.

"Fine. One run. Then you leave me alone."

"But of course."

There was something wrong here, but I couldn't quite figure out what it was.

- - -

At the top of the lift, I slid off to one side, out of the way so I could buckle my boots. Alessandro frowned at me for a second as he got his poles set. Then he said, "Catch me if you can," and was gone.

I cursed under my breath as I finished getting myself set, tugging on my gloves, and grabbing my poles. For a second, I thought about blowing him off completely and going my own way. But I was a little curious. Mom had always said he was an amazing skier. I followed him as he disappeared over the ridge.

When I got to the top of the ridge, I stopped. It was easy to spot Alessandro. He was wearing all black, and although he wasn't wearing a hat, his salt and pepper hair almost made the black go head to toe.

He was impressive—something I would never tell him. He reminded me of the old James Bond movie that opens with the ski scene. He was so smooth, his knees and boots could have been lashed together. It didn't look like he planted his poles so much as just tapped them down.

Shaking my head, I jumped off the rim and headed down the slope. I was able to catch him quickly. I just stayed a few feet directly behind, trying to copy him, turning when he did. I studied his form, watching how his turns seemed to come from the hip instead of the legs.

As a result, I almost ran into him when he pulled up.

Fortunately, the new skis had good edges. I went around him and below him and managed to carve to a stop.

"You need to work on your reflexes," he said.

"You shouldn't stop without warning like that!"

"Your reflexes are slow."

"The gates don't move," I retorted. "I don't ski around moving targets!"

"No," he said agreeably, "they don't. But if you practice with moving targets, then your skiing will be that much better."

"That's stupid," I grumbled.

"Think of the track stars. They run miles at practice and then only race a few hundred yards. You must do more to be better at doing less."

I had to consider that. "Okay. In a weird way that makes sense."

"Ready to try again?"

I gestured down the hill. "After you."

Grinning, he headed off, and I followed in his tracks.

We stopped three more times, and each time, he gave me something else to think about. The last time, he told me to take the lead.

"Why?"

"I want to see how you love the mountain."

"Excuse me?"

"You must love the mountain to ski her," he said.

"Arrgghh! Enough of the sappy crap!"

"I am not being 'sappy.' Without a love of the mountain, you will never be able to ski like a champion."

"Got news for you—I already do." And I pushed off. I was mad at him and at myself. I couldn't believe he would dare to tell me how to ski. But that wasn't as bad as the fact that I was actually listening to his advice.

As I pulled to a stop in front of the lift line, I saw LeMoyne standing by the ski racks.

Thank God, I thought. Now I can ditch Alessandro. I looked back over my shoulder. He was still thirty feet behind me. I always skied fastest when I was pissed.

My feeling of relief evaporated as LeMoyne walked over to me, without his skis and poles. Then I noticed he wasn't wearing his ski boots anymore, either.

Alessandro got to me first, skidding to a stop and sending a light spray of snow on me from my knees down. "You quit concentrating," he accused. "You were too worried about speed and forgot about form."

"Skiing ain't like figure skating. Form doesn't count."

"Better form will give you better speed and control."

LeMoyne stopped just behind me, trying to give us a polite amount of space. "Look," I said, "we did our run, okay? Now I'm going to ski with my friend."

Alessandro nodded and turned for the lift line. I looked over my shoulder at LeMoyne, and he stepped forward the last couple of feet.

"I gotta go home," LeMoyne said apologetically.

"You really left your inhaler there."

"No," he said, shaking his head. "Dad left a message with Kolton. He needs me to come home for something."

"Did he say what?"

"No." I could tell LeMoyne was nervous, and I could

guess why. If his dad was leaving messages at work on LeMoyne's day off, then he was really trying to find him.

"You could probably catch him," LeMoyne said, indicating Alessandro.

"It's all right," I said. "I'd rather ski alone."

"See ya, man," he said, reaching out to shake my hand.

"Yeah. Call me, and let me know what's goin' on, okay?"

"Yeah." He turned to leave, and I headed for the lift.

I rode up on a chair with a couple of retirees who were up from Denver for the day. They said hello, and then pretty much spent the rest of the ride looking at the trail map and discussing their plan. I didn't mind. It gave me some time to think.

As we neared the top, I began watching the skiers on the run under us with interest, but I didn't see the man in black. When I got off the lift, I quickly buckled up and headed for the closest diamond. If fate wanted me to ski with Alessandro, I'd find him.

He was waiting for me at the top of the run.

14

"Phil! Let's go!"

Sirocco yelled back, "In a second!"

Risty shook his head and muttered something to Eliot that I couldn't make out. The bus was running, and everyone else was onboard. Sirocco was standing outside, talking to one of the girls from Winter Park.

"*Now*, Phil!" Risty shouted again.

Ever since Sirocco's father had stormed into the principal's office two weeks ago and demanded his son's instant return to the team's starting lineup, refusing to make him stay in for detention, there had been an ongoing power struggle between Mr. Risty and Sirocco. Sirocco did his best to break every rule that he could.

The whole team was tense and splintered into factions. LeMoyne and I were our own faction. Sirocco and I had done a pretty good job of not talking at all, or even looking at each other, since the incident in the gym. It helped, of course, that he didn't bother coming to any practices that weren't on the slope.

Sirocco climbed on the bus, and Risty started to drive away before Sirocco was seated. He almost fell before he sat next to Tangley. There was some general laughter from his crowd, and I was sure that they were talking about his latest conquest. I wondered if he still talked to Angela; then I resolutely pushed the thought away.

I hadn't heard from her, so I clung to the belief that she did not have Caller ID. In the quiet of my room, I had tried to piece the phone number back together. But the number had been blurry to begin with, and I had done a very effective job of shredding it.

"You goin' to the party?" LeMoyne asked. Risty had decided that we needed a "team-building" party. State was just four weeks away.

"Nah. I'm headin' home."

"Why?"

"I'm tired of hangin' around with a bunch of people who can't even talk to each other."

LeMoyne laughed. "What are you gonna tell Risty?"

"That I've got to get my grades up."

"What? You've slipped to a B?"

I laughed, but the truth was that I was closer to Cs in three of my classes. I had done more partying and eating out in the last four weeks than I had in the last four years. My bank account was lower than it had been in years, too. But I would rather party and spend money than stay home.

Alessandro was there too much.

We skied together once a week now, but that was the only place I was able to handle conversations with him.

The rest of the time, he was too pompous and dreamy. The mushy junk kept pouring out of his mouth, and I had finally realized it wasn't an act—he really felt that way.

I kept skiing with him, though. Risty was able to give me general ideas on what to work on, but Alessandro was able to give me specifics on how to get the finesse that kept chipping away time from my races. Alessandro didn't know that. He hadn't come to another race.

We had family dinners every night—better take-out food than I was used to—but the forced togetherness made it hard to swallow at first. Things had gotten easier, though.

Alessandro still wasn't working, but he was doing stuff around the house. He did laundry, cleaned, and had repaired the lopsided coffee table. He even went grocery shopping, although he never remembered to get the cereal I liked.

Alessandro and Mom had taken off for two "weekend retreats," and, fortunately, I wasn't invited. I worried about Mom's job. She was taking more time off than I thought she should.

I was worried about LeMoyne, too. His parents were talking seriously about moving. "Five card draw?" he asked now, dealing out the cards and helping me deal Alessandro out of my head.

LeMoyne and I played cards for the rest of the ride back to our school. As we pulled into the parking lot, Eliot stood up. "All right, folks, listen up for a minute. You all did a good job today. In addition to Phil, Sandro, Alan, Michelle, and Tara, we've now got Pam, Justine, and Chase qualified for State." Eliot paused for our cheers. "You deserve a reward, and we expect to see all of you at Pete's Pizza Place in an hour."

Risty parked the bus, and everyone began filing off.

"Hey, my mom's here," LeMoyne said, scanning the parking lot. "We can give you a ride home."

"I gotta pick some stuff up at the grocery store," I said. "Thanks, anyway."

"You sure?"

"Yeah. I'll see ya at practice tomorrow," I said as he picked up his duffel bag and started off the bus. I waited till everyone else was gone, and then approached Risty.

"Good job today," he said. "We'll see you in an hour."

"Actually, I'm not going to be at the pizza party."

"Why not?"

"I've got three tests next week and a few missing assignments."

He raised his eyebrows. "You expect me to believe you're going to do homework on a Friday night?"

"It's the only time I have. I'm working all weekend." I shrugged. "And I never realized that missing the whole day for a meet could put me so far behind. I've got a hole to dig out of in a few classes."

"I've told everyone to stay up with classwork and bring books to the meets." Before I could say anything, he added, "But I know how hard it is to do work while at the meets. And it's really hard on those of you who ski at all of them, but that's your fault for being so good," he said with a grin. "You know, you've got a real chance at the State title."

"Only if I can beat Siro—Phil."

"Anything can happen on the slopes, as you've seen in the last few weeks."

"I'm glad our next meet is here. I'm tired of traveling."

"Being on the home mountain's always a good feeling."

I nodded and began down the steps off the bus.

"Hey, Sandro," Eliot said, "how are things with your mom and dad?"

I hesitated but then kept going without answering. After that first meet, Alessandro and Mom had gone into school to put his name on all the paperwork. They made a big fuss about him being able to drive me home from any competitions or pick me up from school.

But he hadn't been to another meet. I didn't know why it bugged me so much—especially since I didn't like spending time with him—but I couldn't get it out of my mind.

I was hoping the apartment lights would be off when I got home, but they were all on. Mom and Alessandro apparently would be home for the weekend. And Alessandro would want a full account of the meet. I reshouldered my backpack as I trudged up the stairs.

I had just reached the second landing when our apartment door flew open.

"Alessandro!" Mom cried, practically leaping out. When she saw me, her face crumpled, and she turned to go back inside. It was a small consolation that she didn't pull the door shut behind her.

It was my intent to just go straight back to my room. Whatever was going on, I didn't want to know. But Mom was curled up on the couch, clutching the phone, and sobbing.

In all our years of scraping by, I had never seen her cry like that.

I dropped my backpack on the floor and walked over to the couch, and then I just stood there. I didn't have a clue what to do. Her sobs began to slow down.

"Mom," I started, reaching out to touch her back.

"Go away," she moaned into the cushions.

Even though that was exactly what I wanted to do, I stayed put. "What's wrong?" I asked.

"Nothing."

"Mom, are you okay?" I asked stupidly.

"I don't need your gloating right now."

An icicle seemed to pierce my midsection. "Where's Alessandro?"

This time, she started bawling. There was no way she'd be able to speak for several minutes.

At a loss, I began walking around our small apartment living room and dining area. As far as I could tell, everything was the same. It wasn't neat, but it was clean. There were a couple of dishes and magazines on the table, and Mom's jacket was hanging from the back of the chair. It didn't look like anything traumatic had happened.

I glanced down the hall, into my room. Everything looked normal there, too.

Mom's crying was an expression of pure pain. I wasn't sure what was causing it, although I was afraid I had a pretty good idea. I grabbed the box of tissues from the counter and took it over to the couch. I felt like I should make sure she saw it, but I was afraid of touching her, so I set it on the floor by her feet.

Then I just sat and waited.

She cried for a long time, long enough that I almost drifted off to sleep. When she finally sat up and put the tissues on her lap, I had to prop myself back up. I watched her blow her nose a half-dozen times, dropping the tissues on the floor. Then she wiped her eyes with a couple more, and only succeeded in making her mascara look like a raccoon's mask.

When her sniffles were almost a minute apart, and her eyes seemed to have stopped leaking, I took a chance. "Mom? What's wrong?"

For a second, I thought I had just succeeded in setting her off again. But she drew a quavering breath and seemed to pull herself together. "He left."

Even expecting it, hearing it said so baldly made my stomach cramp again.

"He left," she repeated as if I hadn't heard.

I wanted to say something, but I was afraid of the strange rock in my throat.

"Sandro, he left us."

It occurred to me that she was going to keep saying this until I acknowledged that I had heard her. "I'm sorry," I said.

"No, you're not," she said bitterly.

"I am, though. I'm sorry he left you."

"He left *us*."

I ignored the impulse to repeat that he had left *her*, not me. Instead, I asked, "Where did he go?"

"I don't know."

"When did he leave?"

"I don't know."

I looked around the apartment again. It still looked the same. It hadn't changed when he came, and it hadn't changed when he left. "What did he say? Or did he just leave a note?"

"He didn't say anything."

I blinked. "He was here last night," I said slowly.

She sniffed and blew her nose again.

"Mom, how do you know he's gone?"

"He's gone."

"Are you sure he didn't just go somewhere for the day?"

"He's gone."

"Mom," I said, "how do you know? If he didn't say anything, and he didn't take anything—"

"He took some clothes."

"All of them?"

"A lot of them."

I rubbed my forehead. "Mom—"

"He left," she moaned, falling on the couch again. "He left, and he's not coming back!"

While she started crying again, I got up and went back to my room. Shutting my door, I leaned back against it. Mom had always had a flair for the dramatic, but this was over the top. Alessandro would probably come home in the next hour or two, bringing dinner from some restaurant as usual.

I turned on my stereo. I didn't want her crying—or his return—to distract me from my homework.

- - -

My alarm clock went off at 6 A.M. on Saturday, and I groaned. I turned it off and stared at it, watching the seconds tick by, and tried to decide if it would be okay to skip practice. It would be fine, except that I was supposed to meet LeMoyne, and he'd stand on that corner waiting for me. That wouldn't be cool. So I pulled myself out of bed and got dressed.

I grabbed my gym bag and went to the kitchen. Passing the living room sofa, I stopped. Mom was still sprawled on it, tissues covering the floor and cushions around her.

Sighing, I went back to her bedroom. It was fine. It didn't look like Alessandro had packed in a hurry or tossed anything around. I pulled the comforter from her bed and took it back to the living room.

As I spread it over her, she mumbled something and shifted, but she didn't wake up.

I waited ten minutes at the corner, but LeMoyne never showed up. I thought about going to his house to drag his butt out of bed, but I was already late for practice. If I was going to practice, I'd have to go by myself. I cussed LeMoyne out in my mind the whole time I did weights and ran. But in a strange way, it was actually nice to have someone other than my mother to be pissed at.

When I walked into the ski shop, the back office door was closed. I tossed my jacket on the chair behind the register, and Robert and I started getting the reserved skis ready.

A few moments later, LeMoyne came out of the office. I

was getting a few sets of poles, and I was confused when he headed straight for the door. He was gone before I could say anything.

Kolton was leaning in the office doorway, staring at the door. I walked over.

"Where'd LeMoyne go?" I asked.

He looked at me in surprise. "He didn't tell you?"

"No."

Looking back at the door, Kolton hesitated, and then said, "Then I guess I shouldn't, either."

"But—"

Shaking his head, Kolton turned and went back into the office.

"What was that all about?" Robert asked me.

"Don't know. We the only ones in here today?" I asked. I exaggerated my worried voice, but I was a little concerned. It was Saturday, and it would get too busy for just the three of us.

"I think Jade and Courtney are working, too."

Courtney had been hired just a couple weeks ago. Since she pretty much had picked up the shifts I had dropped for the ski team, I hadn't worked with her yet. "What's she like?"

"She ain't like Jade," Robert said. Whether that was good or bad, he left for me to decide.

The girls came in all of three minutes before we opened, so I didn't get a chance to talk to either of them. Then, when things slowed down, they hung out by themselves, leaving me and Robert alone. During lunch I called

LeMoyne and asked if I could stop by on my way home. He said "sure," but he didn't offer any explanation or an apology for this morning.

As soon as we closed, the girls clocked out and were gone. They didn't stick around to see what anyone was doing or to invite us to where they were going. Robert was very disappointed. I was kind of relieved. Things had been a little awkward between me and Jade lately, and I wasn't sure why.

Walking over to LeMoyne's house, I almost decided to bail out and just go home. He hadn't included me in whatever was going on; who was I to come barging over? I was his best friend, that's who. And I was pissed that he'd talked to Kolton before he talked to me. I walked too fast, and stopped at the corner to finish my cigarette.

LeMoyne's mom answered the door, looking rather frazzled. "Hi, Sandro. He's back in his room," she said, waving her hand that way as she headed down the stairs. It was the first time since I had known her that she didn't ask how I was or offer to get me some cookies.

"Hey, man. Where were—" I broke off. I had expected to see him chilling on his bed or something. Instead, he was practically buried in the back of his closet, surrounded by boxes and piles of clothes. "What the hell is this?"

"Hey," he said tossing a pair of high-tops into the nearest box and coming back into the room. "You had dinner?"

"Shop just closed," I said. "Which you would have known if you had been there."

"Let's go get somethin' to eat."

"LeMoyne," I warned.

"I know," he said. "But I've gotta get out of here." He grabbed his jacket, and I followed him back to the front door. "Goin' for dinner! Back in an hour!" He yelled down the stairs.

"You going to get pizza?" his mom yelled back.

He glanced at me, and I shrugged. "Sure!"

"Bring one back for us?"

"Pepperoni okay?"

"Sounds great. Do you need some money?" his dad called back up.

"You can pay me back later!"

"Okay!"

We walked almost a block in silence.

"I'm movin'," he said finally.

Although the boxes had made that pretty obvious, I was still a little hurt. "You were gonna skip town without tellin' me?"

"Nah, man. I wouldn't do that. Just . . . It's all happenin' so fast. And—" he shook his head. "And I know how bad you want out of Borealis."

"I knew how bad you wanted the ski team," I said. "Seems like we're gettin' what the other wants."

"Guess so. Sometimes fate don't get it right."

Ignoring the flutter in my stomach, I pressed the issue that upset me most. "But you weren't gonna tell me."

He gave me a light push on the shoulder. "I hate goodbyes. Besides, I'll be at school on Monday, gettin' records and crap."

"So what's happenin'?" I asked as we grabbed a booth.

"My dad got this job in Boulder. He interviewed on Thursday, and they called yesterday to say they want him to start on Tuesday." He shook his head. "I can't believe how fast it happened. I mean, Dad said he was gonna look for a job, like a week or two ago, and then bam! He's got a job."

"And you've got to go that fast, too?" I asked. "What about the house? And your mom's job? And college?" LeMoyne had been accepted to all the schools he had applied to, and still hadn't decided on one yet.

"It will probably take a while to sell the house, and Mom's turning in her notice on Monday. As long as I don't fail all my classes, transferring right now won't make any difference."

The waitress came by and we ordered.

"So you could stay a while longer," I said. "Maybe finish the year here?"

He shook his head. "I probably could but, the thing is, I don't want to. I'm tired of not really fitting in here. And if I get enrolled at Boulder High School, I can play baseball for them. The season starts in three weeks."

"We have a baseball team," I said.

"Psshhtt," he said with disgust. "More than half the season's done inside 'cause the field won't be clear of snow, let alone dry."

"We do most of our ski practice inside, too," I pointed out.

"Team practices, yeah, but we're all expected to find

time to get on the mountain on our own. You know that. That's why you've only been workin', what? Two shifts a week instead of five or six? Besides, skiing's individual. Baseball's a team. You gotta have time to practice as a team on the field."

"Yeah. I guess so."

"That's why skiing's the perfect sport for you," he said as the waitress set the pizza slices down in front of us. "It's individual. It's all about you. You don't need anyone else."

"Maybe I'm tired of individual sports."

He looked up at me. "What's up?"

"Nothin'," I said, sprinkling some Parmesan on my pizza.

"No, man, you wouldn't be this bummed just about me movin'," he said.

"You're breakin' my heart, and you know it," I said. It was our old joke, but in this instance it was true. LeMoyne was the closest thing I had ever had to a brother.

"Well that sounds only fair," Jade said, appearing beside me. Then she was sliding in on my side of the booth.

"What do you mean?" I asked, scooting over.

"After you broke my heart, somebody's gotta break yours." She grabbed my knee and prevented me from scooting farther away.

"I didn't break your heart, Jade," I said, trying to keep the joking tone. "I just didn't let you break mine."

Courtney sat down next to LeMoyne. He didn't move over very far, and she didn't seem to mind. I wondered if she was keeping his knee hostage, too.

Jade pulled a slice of pepperoni off my pizza and popped it in her mouth. "So what's been with you all day?"

"Nothin'," I said.

"You've been real quiet," Courtney said, helping herself to some of LeMoyne's pizza.

"How would you know?" I demanded.

"You haven't been yourself," Jade continued, as if Courtney hadn't spoken.

I pushed away from her and turned sideways in the booth, preventing her from closing in on me again. "You have no idea who I am," I retorted. "And you weren't even talking to me today."

LeMoyne smirked. Jade looked hurt. Courtney said, "I bet it's got something to do with his girlfriend."

We all stared at her. "I don't have a girlfriend," I said.

"So who's—" she pulled a piece of paper from her pocket, and I recognized the pink memo pad from the ski shop—"Angela?"

LeMoyne coughed suddenly and violently. I reached for the pink piece of paper, and Courtney held it out of my reach. Just as LeMoyne made a move to help me, she stood up. So did Jade.

Inside, I was fuming. When had Angela been in the shop? Why hadn't Courtney given me the message right away? Jade was looking at it, and Courtney was whispering something to her.

LeMoyne and I looked at each other over our pizza, ignoring the girls.

Jade threw the piece of paper down in the middle of the

table, right in a puddle of soda. "You could have just told me!" she said, then stalked off, Courtney following her.

As I wiped the paper off with a napkin, LeMoyne said, "I thought you didn't get it on with Jade."

"I didn't."

"Wow. Hate to see what she does to guys she's serious about."

"No kidding."

"What's the message?"

I glanced at the paper. "Just says her name and number."

"Does it say when she called?"

I hadn't even thought that she would call the shop. "No," I said slowly. "I was thinking she had just dropped by."

"You gonna call her this time?"

I shrugged as I stuffed the paper into my pocket. We finished eating and got a pepperoni to go for LeMoyne's parents. We started walking home in the light snow.

"So what's goin' on?"

"What do you mean?"

"Jade's not always the brightest girl, but she's right this time. You ain't been yourself tonight." He grinned sideways at me. "And I *do* know you."

I kicked a chunk of ice along the sidewalk. "You're leaving. That's enough to bum anyone out."

He laughed and kicked the ice. "Seriously."

"It's Alessandro," I admitted.

"He got a job yet?"

"Don't think so." I kicked the ice, and it went spinning

out into the street where it was squashed by a car. "He took off."

"Oh, crap," LeMoyne stopped short, but I kept walking. He caught up with me quickly. "When did he bail?"

"Yesterday."

"How's your mom doin'?"

"She's a wreck."

"How bad is it?" he asked.

"Don't know yet, but I'm guessing pretty bad."

"What can I—"

I kicked another ice chunk. "He may not even be gone," I said suddenly.

"But you just said—"

"Mom said he bailed yesterday, but he didn't leave a note or anything. And you know how she can blow things out of proportion."

"Yeah. Well, if he did bail, and you need help . . ." he trailed off.

"Thanks, man," I said, forcing a smile. I was pretty sure we were in bad shape, whether Alessandro was still staying with us or not. "But there's not much you can do from Boulder anyway."

"Sandro—"

Closing my eyes against the tears, I shook my head too fast. "Sorry. Didn't mean that. We all gotta do what we gotta do."

And I had to do it on my own. Again.

15

The apartment was dark, so I just flipped on the light as I walked in. There was an immediate moan from the lump under the blanket on the couch.

"Mom?"

Another moan. I flipped off the light and felt my way through the apartment to the kitchen, where I turned on the range light instead.

"Mom, have you **eaten** today?" The sink looked clean. There were take-out boxes in the fridge, but I didn't feel like sorting through them, so I made two peanut-butter-and-jelly sandwiches.

I carried the plates and two cans of soda over to the sofa. "Come on, Mom. Get up and eat." The lump shifted under the blanket, but made no response. "Mom." When she didn't move, I went for blood. "Did Alessandro call?"

The lump of blankets began trembling.

"Maybe he'll call tomorrow." I reached up and flipped the light on again.

"Go away."

"Or maybe he'll pull up in a limo with—"

"Be quiet!"

"—a big sparkling ring and—"

"Sandro!" Mom shrieked, sitting up and pulling the blanket off her face. "Shut up!"

"Oh, good, you're up." I pushed the sandwich toward her. "Eat."

She glared at me with red, swollen, puffy eyes. "I can't."

"You can."

"My heart's broken."

"Again."

"You bastard."

"Not my fault," I pointed out. "*He* left *again*. Not my fault. Pick up and go on, Mom. It's what you do."

"I can't," she whispered, tears streaming once again.

"You have to."

"Can't!"

I bit into my sandwich.

"Sandro, you have no idea . . ."

I snorted.

"He left us."

Taking a swallow of soda, I said, "Nothing new there."

"It's bad this time, Sandro," Mom said softly, taking a deep breath. "You have no idea how bad."

"You'll survive, Mom. No one's ever died of a broken heart."

"No, but they've died of starvation."

"So eat your sandwich."

"Sandro, we have no money."

"Still not telling me anything I haven't heard before."

"It's gone," she insisted. "I haven't made a Jeep payment for two months, haven't paid any of the utilities . . ."

I was staring at her. "You haven't paid the utilities? Like the gas and phone? For how long?"

She shrugged and poked her finger into the middle of her sandwich.

"How long, Mom? How long till we're sitting in the dark?"

"I don't know if we'll be sitting in the dark or kicked out first."

"You haven't paid rent yet, either?" She shook her head and tears began to slide down her face again. "Why not, Mom? Why in God's name not?"

"I—I—" She fell back down on the couch, lost in her sobs again.

"Where are the bills?"

She was crying too hard to hear me. I grabbed her roughly by the shoulder. "Mom! *Where are the bills?*"

"It doesn't matter—"

"It *does* matter, Mom!"

She buried her face in the blankets and sofa cushions again. I wasn't going to be able to talk to her for a while.

In disgust, I went back to her bedroom, to the small table that she used as a desk. It was always littered with bills. Usually, Mom was pretty good about keeping it somewhat organized, putting the most overdue or important bills first.

It didn't take me long to locate the rent notice. It was on top, a not-too-nasty note informing us that we now owed an additional twenty dollars because we were more than five days late. I checked the date, and discovered that by making payment tomorrow, we could avoid eviction.

Under the rent notice were the electric, phone, and gas bills. I took the electric and gas, and after a moment's hesitation, picked up the phone, too. I wouldn't be able to pay all of it, but maybe I could send enough to stop them from disconnecting our line.

My bank account could handle this. But buying food would take out another big chunk. I was going to have to go back to work and get as many hours at the shop as I could.

As I turned to go, another bill caught my eye. To my surprise, it was a credit card. Mom didn't use credit cards; she had gotten in debt quickly with the few that were in her name when she first got here, and she swore she'd never go in debt again. She had always drilled that into me, too. Her credit cards were simply for emergencies.

I picked up the bill. When I saw the amount due, I abruptly sat down on the edge of her bed. The minimum payment alone was more than our rent. What had happened?

I scanned the items. Restaurants, every day. All-Pro Ski Stop. I winced. That was my skis. Clothing stores. Two hotels.

"Mom!" I shouted as I went back to the living room. "Mom! What the hell is this?"

"Mom?" I asked, leaning down so I could see her face. Her eyes were closed. "You gonna look at this?"

"I can't," she said. "It's totally hopeless."

"Mom, how could you be so stupid?"

"I love him."

"So? You say you love me, and you don't give me your credit card."

She continued as if she hadn't heard me. "I loved him. I loved him."

"Yeah, yeah, tell him when he comes back—"

"He's not coming back, Sandro."

I shrugged. "Whatever. It won't make much difference either way. We're in deep now, and I don't know how to get out." I studied the bill for a moment. "Can you cancel the stuff on the bill?"

"No," she said.

"How about returning the stuff?"

"I might be able to return some of it for credit, but not much."

"Still be better than paying the whole thing," I countered.

"Yeah." She sighed and stared off at the blank wall. "I thought we were soul mates."

"What a load of crap." I shook my head. "Can you work some double shifts this week?"

"I can't work," she whined, lying down again. "I can't do anything! I'm dying of a broken heart."

"You have to work double shifts, so we don't die of starvation out on the streets." I stood up. "I'm going to bed. What time do you want me to get you up tomorrow?"

"I'm sleeping tomorrow."

"I'll call you around noon. Make sure you're up for work."

"I can't work."

"Better go to bed."

"I can't."

"You can," I said, going to my room. "You have to."

I sat down on the edge of my bed for a few moments, holding my head in my hands. Then I stood up and pulled the pink memo-pad paper out of my pocket. I studied it for a few seconds.

Although I was dying to talk to her, find out why she had called—or dropped by—and see if she would be in town soon, I felt that calling her right now would be a really bad idea. I didn't want her to think I only talked about my problems. So I took a roll of tape and stuck the paper to the back of the door.

I could see it when the door was shut; no one else could see it when the door was open. I taped all four edges of the pink page down. It wasn't going anywhere.

Unfortunately, neither was I.

- - -

When I asked Kolton if there were extra shifts I could pick up, he gave me a strange look. "You're already maxed out."

"I'm only pulling like ten hours a week!"

"That's what happens when you're a big ski star."

"I'm quittin' the team."

"You're what?" he asked.

"I'm quittin' the team," I said, surprised how hard it was to actually say the words. "I need more hours. And if I can't get them here, then I'll go someplace else."

"Why're you threatenin' me?" Kolton demanded. "You think that's gonna help?"

I took a deep breath. "I've got trouble, Kolton. I need to make money."

"I'm sorry, but—"

"I can work during the day."

"You got school."

I shrugged. When I had taken the rent in, the landlord had hassled me. Apparently, Mom had been late paying the rent more than a few times. He demanded next month's payment. I was so terrified of being evicted that I gave it to him even though I was pretty sure it was illegal.

Now my checking account was too low. Walking to work, I had come to the conclusion that not only would I have to quit the team, but that I might have to drop out of school all together. Things were so tight, I'd probably have to quit eating breakfasts as well.

"You wanna talk?"

"Nope."

Kolton sighed. "I could use some extra help this week, *after* school. We'll see after that."

"Thanks, man." I turned and headed toward the repair room.

"Sandro, when you're ready to talk—"

I waved, so he would know I heard him, but I didn't say anything. My throat was so tight I felt like I was choking. As soon as I got to the repair room, I shut the door. I hadn't cried in years, and I didn't need anyone seeing me.

Twenty minutes later, when I finally came back out to the register, we were open and had a pretty good line going.

I let myself get swept away in work for a few hours. When things slowed down, Kolton asked who wanted to go ski. Robert and Jade both shouted "I do!"

I shook my head. "I'll stick around here," I said, leaning on the counter.

Kolton flipped a coin, and Robert was off to put his skis on while Jade came over to sulk by the counter.

"So," she said.

"So what?"

"We gonna play rummy or just sit around and talk?"

I opened the *Save a Penny*, the local weekly paper, and began skimming it. It didn't offer the news; it carried just ads and classifieds. Want ads, real estate, rental properties, and special services were all covered. There were notices of garage sales and individual items for sale, too. When I saw how cheap used skis were, I had to bite my lip. I wouldn't be able to get a third of what Alessandro—or, rather, Mom—had paid for them.

Kolton, on his way to the office, took the paper out of my hand. "I don't like threats," he said.

"I wasn't looking for another job," I called to him. As his office door swung shut, I added, "Yet."

"So who is she?" Jade asked, shuffling the cards.

I looked up at the empty shop. "Who is who?"

"The girl." At my blank look, she said, "Andrea or whoever."

"Angela?"

"Whatever," she said, shrugging and staring at the cards as she began sorting them.

Sensing I was about to get in trouble but not really sure

why, I said, "She's Angela. She lives in Golden. Why?"

Jade just shrugged again and refused to look up at me. I was about to go try to talk to Kolton when she finally said, "You really like her?"

"What's going on, Jade?" I asked. "I'm totally confused."

"I thought you didn't believe in love," she said.

"Right."

"So what's so special about her?"

"I didn't say there was anything special about her."

"You didn't have to. It's all over your face whenever you talk about her."

"I don't talk about her. You brought her up."

"When Courtney gave you that message last night . . ."

I waited, but Jade seemed to have stopped. "What about it? It was a phone number."

"Your face . . . I can just tell she means a lot to you."

"You weren't even there!" I exclaimed in bewilderment. "You were walking away and couldn't see anything."

"I didn't have to. Just the fact that she called—"

Jade had been flipping the cards over, stacking them face-up on the counter. I was startled when a tear landed right in the middle of the queen of hearts.

"Jade," I said slowly, "you're a really great—"

"Stop!" she practically shouted. "Stop right there!" She looked up at me, eyes welling up. "I don't want to hear how 'great a friend' I am!"

"I wasn't going to—I mean, you *are* a great friend, but that's not what I was going to say."

Her head was bent down again, and I couldn't see her

face. The bells above the shop door rang, and I looked over to see a father bringing in his daughter, carrying her skis. Jade scooped up the cards and bolted for the back of the store.

I helped readjust the binding for the girl, and then someone else came in, looking for his misplaced hat. Robert came back, and he asked Jade to play rummy. There was a rather steady flow of people right before our afternoon rush started, and then we closed up. Jade was gone before I could talk to her.

I headed home, but then decided to detour to the lodge. When I had called home at noon, no one had answered. I assumed Mom was at work, but something told me to check. She wasn't there, and the other bartender was pissed.

While I walked home, I tried to get my anger under control. Mom had just had her heart broken, I reminded myself. She was really depressed. I shouldn't be too hard on her.

But when I walked in the front door and saw her still on the couch, my rage boiled over.

"Get up!" I yelled. "You were supposed to be at work two hours ago!"

She whimpered.

"Get your ass off the sofa and get a life!"

"It's not that easy," she moaned.

I grabbed her arms and pulled her up. She swayed, not trying at all to stand. Half-carrying, half-dragging her, I got her into her bathroom. I opened the shower door, and then pushed her in.

"What are you—" she began just as I turned the water on.

She screeched. "That's cold!"

"Give it a minute."

"I'm still dressed!" She tried to get out of the shower stall.

"You've been wearing those clothes for three days now. They need to be washed." I shut the door on her.

"Sandro!"

"Get it together, Mom. You need to go to work." In her room, I dug through the dresser and closet until I found something she could wear. I took them back to the bathroom and tossed them inside. Before I pulled the door shut, I said, "We've got bills to pay. You can't lose your job now."

16

The next few days melted into a blur. I went to the ski shop the minute the last bell rang. As soon as the shop closed, I went home. The apartment was empty. Although it should have felt more like the home I knew, I guess I had gotten used to Alessandro being around. If I wasn't careful, I could almost imagine I missed him.

The person I *did* miss was LeMoyne. He came to school on Monday as promised, but not for long. He just went to each of his teachers, turned in textbooks, and got his grades signed off. We only got to talk for a few seconds before he left, which, I think, was actually a good thing. I didn't want to really say good-bye to him. He gave me his new phone number, and said I could call any time, even collect if I wanted to.

Jade was a puzzle. I kept catching her staring at me, but she only talked to me at work when she had to. From what Robert and Courtney said, though, she had a whole lot of hot dates, so I didn't worry about her too much.

At least Mom was working again. I called the lodge

every couple of hours, asked if she was there, and if they said "yes," I just said "thanks" and hung up. I didn't need to talk to her; I just needed to know that she was keeping on with her life.

The only interesting thing to happen on Tuesday was Alan Webster seeking me out during lunch. He wanted to know why I had missed practice on Monday, and I told him that something important had come up. He just told me about some of the stupid and useless things that had happened at practice, and then Sirocco and Tangley came into the cafeteria. So Webster said he'd see me later and headed off to meet them. I didn't bother to tell him that the "something" wasn't going away, and I wouldn't be at practice any more.

On Wednesday, the phone was ringing when I got home, but by the time I got the door open and dropped my bag by the front door, it stopped. Once again, I wished we could afford an answering machine or Caller ID, or to use *69. I waited by the phone for at least five minutes, but it didn't ring again.

I decided it was time for me to take a chance, and I went back to my room. I really didn't need to look at the pink paper on the door (I had the number memorized), but I wanted to check it one more time. I sat down, wiped my hands on my jeans, and then picked up the phone and dialed as fast as I could.

It started to ring right away, and I resisted the urge to hang up before anyone answered.

On the third ring, someone said, "Hello," and I said, "Hello, is Angela—" before I realized the person was still talking. "—and we're sorry to miss your call. Please leave a message, so we don't have to miss your information!"

Then the tone sounded, and I hung up. As soon as I did, I was mad at myself. I could have just left a message, and then if she really wanted to talk to me, *she* could call *me* back. I wouldn't have to do the dialing . . . or pay for the call.

As I made myself some spaghetti for dinner, I tried to analyze the voice on the machine. It had sounded a little like Angela, I thought, but not quite right. Maybe it was her big sister. Then I wondered if she had her own phone line, or if she and her family used the same answering machine.

I began planning what I would say when I called her back. I would have to call as soon as I finished eating, so I could just leave a message. And in case her parents and everyone else could hear, it would have to sound good.

I decided that, in this case, simple was better. So I'd just say who I was, ask for Angela, and leave my phone number.

Quickly, I picked up the phone again and dialed.

"Hello?"

I waited for the rest of the message.

"Hello?"

Startled, I said, "Hey!"

"Who's this?"

"I'm . . . this is . . . Is Angela there?" I blurted.

"No, she's not."

"Oh."

The person on the other end didn't say anything.

"Thank you," I said in a rush, and slammed down the phone. It had been a long time since I had felt that stupid. I picked up the phone and dialed the first four digits of LeMoyne's number before I remembered it wasn't his number anymore. I hung up. Almost instantly, the phone rang again.

I couldn't answer it. It was probably Angela. She probably did have Caller ID, or could afford to *09 the phone calls whenever she wanted to. But I didn't want to listen to the phone ring, either. I unplugged the phone and spent the rest of the evening doing my homework in silence.

- - -

On Thursday, during English class, Mr. Risty came to get me. He whispered to Mrs. DeLapp first, and then said, "Sandro, I need to see you for a minute."

I followed him out to the hall and watched him shut the door to the classroom behind us. Then he turned and faced me, arms crossed over his chest.

"What?"

"Where have you been?" he asked.

"Something came up. I can't make practices."

"And you can't come tell me this? You can't come talk to me? You just quit showing up?"

I shrugged, but I couldn't look at him. I had known it was a crappy way to treat him, but I had been trying to avoid this conversation.

"Sandro, State is in three weeks. You can't just give up right now."

"I'm not."

"You can't just give up on your teammates right now,

either. They're depending on you and Phil to lead us to our first championship in years!"

"They've still got Sirocco," I said.

"Sandro—"

"Look, I'm not exactly happy about this, either," I said. He leaned against one of the lockers. "What's going on?"

"Nothin'," I said, staring down the hallway.

"If you quit because of a crisis of some sort, talk to me, and maybe we can work something out. But if you quit because of nothing, Sandro, that's really sad."

"I just can't ski anymore."

"Sandro—"

"I'm sorry, Mr. Risty. I really am. But I can't. And I can't talk anymore, either. I've got a test tomorrow, and I need to get back in there."

"If you quit now," he said slowly, "I won't let you come back in a week or two."

I thought about saying I'd just get Mr. Sirocco to come in and make the principal put me back on the team, but I didn't. "Don't worry about that. I'm not coming back," I said. I walked back into my English class, but I didn't hear anything Mrs. DeLapp had to say. All I could think of was Saturday. Not only was it our last regular meet, but it was also a home meet.

I was scheduled to work all day Saturday. I needed the money, so I had to be there. But the racecourse was going to be visible through the big picture window in the ski shop. Even if I didn't watch, everyone else would, and I'd be hearing about it.

And the State Championships were in three weeks. Even without the last meet of the season, I was qualified and expected to place in the top six. I was so upset about the ski team I couldn't focus on anything Thursday night.

I was pretty sure I failed the English test on Friday. I probably also failed the pop quizzes that my math and science teachers decided to give, since I hadn't done any of the homework at all.

When I got home that evening, I was surprised to see the apartment lights on. As I climbed the stairs, I thought about all the things I was going to say to Alessandro, all the things I was going to shout at him. By the time I reached the last set of steps, I was taking them two at a time.

I was shocked when I flung the door open and saw Mom sitting on the couch by herself. Then I realized what had just happened. For the first time, I had gotten sucked into her dream, sucked into her belief that Alessandro was really going to come back.

I had to take a couple of deep breaths to settle myself down again.

"What are you doing?" I finally asked.

"Watching TV," she said, tossing a piece of popcorn in her mouth.

"Why aren't you at work?"

"Who made you my keeper?" she snapped.

"You did," I retorted, "when you let everything get torn apart, and I had to pick up the tatters."

She grabbed the remote and turned up the volume.

Turning the TV off crossed my mind, but I was just too tired to deal with her. Still, I didn't want to stay home with her, either.

I put my backpack in my bedroom and then went back out and picked up the phone. There wasn't a dial tone. I stared at the phone in confusion for a second. I almost asked Mom if the phone service had been cut off, when I suddenly remembered. Even though Mom was focused on the TV and oblivious to what I was doing, I felt my face flush as I plugged the phone back in. Lifting the handset, I was rewarded with a dial tone. I dialed quickly.

"Hello?"

"Hey, Kolton. It's Sandro."

"Hey, Sandro. What's up?"

"Nothin'. What're you and Torey doin' tonight?"

"I think we were just gonna watch a flick. You wanna come over?"

"Yeah," I said, glad he had offered instead of making me ask. "See ya in a few."

"See ya."

I hung up, and Mom said, "Where are you going?"

"Out," I said, putting my coat back on.

"Where?"

"Tell ya what," I said, opening the front door. "Let's pretend you're working on a normal Friday night when the tips are really good, and you don't have a clue where I am." And I stepped out into the cold night.

- - -

I was fighting a big headache the next morning. Kolton and Torey had rented a couple of really cheesy high-school movies, and had a bottle of rum and a two-liter of Coke. After I told Kolton and Torey about the drama my life had become, Kolton fixed me the first strong drink of the night, and Torey didn't even make a face at him. As a result, I had crashed on the couch at Kolton's and then gone into work with him. He made me shower and then lent me some clean clothes, telling me he didn't want me to be smelly and bother the customers.

The main rush was over. There were a couple of stragglers being helped by Robert and Courtney. Jade was on the schedule, but she hadn't shown up yet. Kolton had muttered about firing her again a couple of times, and then had called her. I'm not sure what was said, but he quit threatening. When I asked when she'd be in, he said she was staying home for the day.

When the door opened, I turned to welcome the new customer and then froze. A horrible feeling of déjà vu swept over me as I saw my mom. At least Alessandro wasn't there, too.

As I opened my mouth to say hello, she yelled, "Where the hell were you last night?"

Everyone in the shop turned to stare. I was mortified. But she wasn't done.

"How dare you do that to me! You have no right to just walk out like that! You have no right to leave me alone all night, wondering where you are!" By now she was right in front of me, but she continued to yell. In fact, she was getting so loud she was close to screaming. "I was up all night! I had no idea! You could have been anywhere! I kept waiting and waiting! But you didn't come home. I went to your ski meet and you weren't there. . . ." Her voice finally broke, and the screams turned to a whisper with frightening speed. "You left, and then you didn't come home. You didn't come back!"

The shop was utterly silent. Kolton moved to her side and put his arm around her shoulders as she almost dissolved into tears. He steered her around the counter, and as they moved into his office, I heard her sobs begin.

For a few seconds I just stood there, staring in shock at the place where my mother had just been. A hand came down on my shoulder, and I jumped.

"You okay?" Robert asked quietly.

I nodded and realized that the shop was still silent because everyone was still staring at me.

"Maybe you should go to the office," Robert suggested.

"Yeah," I said. "Good idea."

As I walked to the office, I could hear gentle mumbling from the people in the store as they resumed talking, but I couldn't hear what they were saying. I stopped just outside the office. I knew I had to go in, but I didn't want to. My mother was not the same person I had known. Ever since Alessandro had returned, she had been different—lively, happy, almost shining with joy. And when he left, she had spiraled so quickly out of control that I had no idea what to expect from her.

I didn't hear any sobbing from inside, so maybe Kolton had been able to get her to settle down. I closed my eyes for a long second, and then I stepped inside the office.

Mom was slumped in Kolton's chair, hair covering her face. He was kind of kneeling in front of her, patting her knee and saying, "It'll be okay. Everything's all right. You're gonna be fine," over and over again.

I wondered if it was true.

It only took three steps to get to her, but it seemed like they were huge leaps. I put my hand on her shoulder, and felt her shaking. Kolton glanced up at me, nodded, and then stood up and left the office, quietly shutting the door behind him.

"Mom—"

"I'm sorry!" she burst out. "Sandro, I'm so sorry! So sorry!"

"It's okay, Mom," I said. "I'm sorry, too."

She sniffled, and I thought she was pulling herself together. Then she said, "I thought you had left me, too." She started trembling. "I thought you were finally sick of me and you left me, too."

"No, Mom," I said. "I didn't leave you."

"Why not? I can't pay the bills. I don't help you with school. I don't see you ski. I don't even know who your friends are! Why would you want to stay?"

"Because you're my mom," I said, stroking the top of her head. "And even though sometimes you do stupid things—"

"I always do stupid things!" she wailed.

"Sometimes," I emphasized. "You *sometimes* do stupid things. But that doesn't make you a bad person."

She sniffled again. "I thought you had left me, too," she repeated.

"I'm not Alessandro, Mom. I'm nothing like him."

"But—"

"Don't," I said. "Please don't ever compare me to him again."

"Why aren't you skiing?"

"I quit."

"Why?"

I just stared at her for a long second.

"Oh," she said. Then, "Oh! Oh, God, Sandro, how much more of your life can I screw up?"

"It's okay, Mom."

"No, it's not. How can you even say that?"

"I didn't want to ski on the team in the first place, remember?"

She was quiet, and I waited for her to argue with me some more. But then, softly, she said, "You're right. He's gone. But you're not. And I'm not going to waste any more time waiting for him. We're moving."

"We're what?"

"We're going to do what you've always wanted to do. We're moving."

"Where?"

"I don't know yet."

"When?"

"Soon. Now. End of the month."

"Mom," I began. "We can't just pick up and go."

She stood up and used her fingertips to wipe the last of the tears from under her eyes. "Yes, we can." She sniffed one last time and then tried to smile.

"Mom, he still might—"

"Don't," she said sharply. "Don't fall into my trap. He's not coming back and we just have to accept that."

"But we can't just leave!" How many times had I dreamed of doing just that? Why was I arguing now?

"Give Kolton your two weeks' notice. I'll go turn mine in right now."

She was gone from the room before I could say anything or stop her. Groaning, I dropped into Kolton's chair. A few seconds later, he came into the office.

"Your mom just gave me your two weeks' notice."

Now it was my turn to slump in the chair. "I know."

"First, you're demandin' extra hours, and now you're sayin' you're leavin'. That ain't very fair."

"I'm sorry, Kolton. Things are kinda screwed up right now."

He nodded but didn't say anything.

"I'm tryin' to be straight with you." I took a deep breath. "I'm sorry about the scene she caused." I was dying for a cigarette. But I was down to two cigarettes a day and was saving money. If I could quit smoking now, at least the ski season wouldn't be a complete loss.

"It's all right. What happened?"

"Just what you saw. She freaked." I leaned back in the chair and scrubbed at the top of my head. "I wish I knew what to do."

"He's really not coming back?"

"Nope."

"That's too bad. I thought the three of you had a real chance to be a family."

Robert stuck his head in the doorway. "Hey, Sandro, there's someone here to see you."

"Not another blubbering female?"

He grinned. "She's not blubbering yet."

Kolton and I exchanged glances. I stood up and tried to beat Kolton to the door, but he had a head start. He and Robert were both in the doorway, and I had to peer between them.

Angela was standing at the counter, examining the assortment of lip balms in the basket.

"You dog," Robert said to me in an undertone. "You got Jade *and* her eatin' out of your hand."

I pushed him out of the way and went to the counter. I had a huge stupid grin on my face, and I couldn't seem to get rid of it. "Angela!"

She looked up with a grin that was just as goofy as mine.

"I came to see your race," she said. "But your name's not on the board, and Alan said you're not on the team anymore."

Hundreds of questions whirled through my head, but all I said was, "Alan's right."

"Oh."

Suddenly, I realized that I had sounded kind of short, so I added, "I had to quit the team. Family problems. How'd you know I was supposed to be skiing today?"

"Your mom said you would be."

"When did you talk to my mom?"

"Last night," she said. "Didn't she tell you I called?"

"We kind of had a stressful morning," I said. "I'm sorry I missed it."

She shrugged. "I was thinking I had the wrong number.

I've been calling for a couple of days, and no one answered it."

I felt my face get hot. "We've had some phone problems, too."

"Oh."

"Ahem," Kolton cleared his throat right behind me. He had a strict rule about socializing with friends during business hours.

"Can I take my lunch break now?" I asked him.

"At nine thirty?" he asked. I just raised my eyebrows at him. "Okay. Yeah. Fine. Just take it somewhere else."

I looked at Angela. "Want to go to lunch?"

She just grinned again, and that was all I needed. I took her hand as we left the shop, and I'm pretty sure I heard Robert whistle a catcall as the door swung shut behind us.

17

"Now what?"

I looked up from my Coke and tried not to grin stupidly. "'Now what' what?" I asked.

"What are you going to do?" Angela asked. Her voice was steady, but her face was a little flushed.

"I'll do what Mom decides to do. I'll either stay here or move. Since I'm not legal yet, I don't get much choice beyond that."

She didn't look away. "Your mom should be—"

"My mom's a mess," I broke in. "She always has been. And now that her dream almost came true before being totally shattered, she's an even bigger mess." I could tell she was mulling this over, and I wanted to cut her off at the pass. "Look, I'm really glad you cared enough to listen to the whole story, but I'm kind of tired of it. Could we talk about something else?"

"Like what?"

"Like how long you'll be up here today."

The pink was back in her cheeks. "I said I'd call if I wouldn't be home for dinner."

"So I could ask you to go out to dinner with me and you might say yes?"

"If you asked, I might."

I had to admit I wouldn't like her as much if she tried to make my life easy. "Will you go out to dinner with me?"

"No."

I blinked. There was a difference between being difficult and being outright mean.

She continued, "I will, however, *take you* out to dinner."

Staring at her, I said, "Maybe I won't go out with you."

It was her turn to look shocked. She recovered a little faster than I had. "Please, Sandro. I'd really like to take you out to dinner."

"Why?"

"Because I like talking to you, and I want to spend more time with you. And I can afford dinner for two right now—you can't."

"But—"

"And if you don't get back to the rental shop fast, you probably won't be able to afford anything at all."

I looked at the watch on her wrist and swore, practically jumping out of my chair. "I gotta go!"

"I know," she replied. "And since you probably need to run all the way there, I think I'll just follow later."

"Okay," I said, edging toward the door.

"When should I come back to the shop?"

"Six thirty."

"See you then," she said, smiling and waving.

I waved back and bolted.

- - -

Laughing, Angela leaned back in her chair. "I can't believe you said that!"

"Why not?" I demanded, toying with the straw wrapper. "I was only six, and that Santa Claus was trippin'."

We were quiet for a moment. Then she said, "Your scar's a lot better," and she reached out but stopped just short of touching my cheek.

"I'll still make a good Frankenstein for Halloween," I said, wondering why my skin was suddenly tingling even though she hadn't touched me.

She pushed the empty plates to one side and pulled my hand toward her, turning it over as she did so.

"What are you doing?"

"I'm going to read your palm."

I tried halfheartedly to get my hand back. "Now *you're* the one trippin'," I said.

"Shh," she said, still grasping my hand and staring at it with intensity. "Um-hmm . . . oh . . . yep, just as I thought."

She relaxed her grip slightly, and I pulled away. "'Just as you thought' what?"

"You will have one true love."

I looked at my hand. "It doesn't say that."

"Yes, it does!"

"Where?" I demanded, pushing my hand back at her.

"Right here," she said, tracing a line on my palm. I tried not to shiver. "You have one very deep, continuous love line. No major branches. And here, your life line—"

"Yeah?"

"You'll be with your love all your life," she said simply, releasing my hand.

"What else does my hand tell you?"

"You have a very deep intellectual line—"

"Hah!" I scoffed.

"It breaks into several small branches here, and then goes back together, see? That means you'll have to choose between all of your talents to decide on one career to follow."

I took my hand back and stared at it. "Looks like a hand to me," I said slowly. Something about the way she shrugged and looked down made me realize I had said the wrong thing. "Where'd you learn this?" I almost added "crap," but stopped myself just in time.

"You don't care," she said.

I couldn't believe how cute she was when she pouted. "I wouldn't ask if I didn't."

She looked up at me. "I like to go to the Renaissance festivals. I've got an aunt who reads palms and Tarot cards for a living."

"I bet you read your horoscope, too."

"Daily," she said seriously. "I knew you were a Sagittarius the first time we met."

"Oh, really?"

She nodded. I was discovering that her green eyes could hypnotize me.

"What's your sign?" I asked, feeling like an actor in a bad movie.

"I'm an Aquarius. We're compatible."

"What?" I asked. The last part had been too muffled.

"Nothing."

"Are you saying our meeting was destined in the stars?"

"Um-hmm. The stars told me I'd meet you that first day."

"Which first day? At the shop? Or on the slopes?"

"At the shop."

"And you knew you were going to meet me?" I asked skeptically.

"I knew I'd meet someone special. And when I saw you . . ." She shrugged. "You don't have to believe me."

"I do, though," I said. "Just because I don't believe in fate doesn't mean I don't think you believe in it."

She looked at her watch. "I need to get going. I told my parents I'd be home by eleven."

"So early?"

"It's a two-hour drive on mountain roads," she said. "My parents weren't real excited about me staying up here this late anyway."

I wondered what it would be like to have parents who cared where you were and when you'd be home. Then I thought about my mother this morning. Maybe it was too late for me to ever accept a real parent.

"Well, let's go then. I don't want you to be late. In fact, it'd be better if you could get home early."

She made a face at me.

"I'm being very serious," I said, grabbing her hand on the table. "I want you to be able to come up here again. Soon."

"But maybe I won't have to," she said. "Maybe next

time, I'll be coming to see you in Denver or Boulder or someplace else."

"Maybe." I didn't care where I saw her again—as long I got to see her.

I walked her out to her car. "Can I give you a ride home?" she asked.

I shook my head. "You need to get home. I'll be mad as hell if you're late and get grounded or somethin'." That was true, but I didn't want her seeing the company housing where I lived, either.

"I've got time to take you home."

"That's all right," I said.

"Don't tell me you're one of those guys that doesn't like female drivers," she said, and from her tone I could tell that a "yes" would get me in trouble.

"Just go on home," I said. "I've got to make a stop anyway."

"What have you got to do this late?"

"Just a couple of things," I said.

"Keeping secrets isn't healthy," she said.

"Go," I said firmly. "You're gonna be late."

"No, I—" The fastest way to get her to quit talking was to kiss her, so I did. She kind of froze for a second, and then she raised her hand. I thought she was going to push me away. Instead, she just rested her hand on my chest.

When the kiss stopped, she stepped back and said, "Call me." Then she got into her car and drove away.

18

When I saw the lights on in our apartment, I hesitated. Mom was up, and that was a good thing. The question was what kind of mood she was in. There was a note taped to our front door from our neighbor, saying she had signed for a delivery. I pulled it down and opened the door into chaos.

"What's going on?" I asked.

"I'm packing," she said.

I looked around. Our few personal belongings had all been pulled out of the drawers. Some of them were in boxes, some in plastic bags, but most were just strewn all over the floor. "You're packing?"

"Yes. I gave my notice at work and to the landlord today. We'll be out of here in two weeks."

"And where are we going?" I asked, sitting on the back of the couch. "Where are you going to work? Where are we going to live?"

"I don't know yet," she said airily.

"You don't know? *You don't know?* How can you—" I was so mad I didn't know how to continue.

"Sandro, you're the one who's wanted to get out of here for a long time. What are you complaining about now?"

"We can't just *go*, Mom. We have to have some kind of plan, some kind of . . . of . . . security."

She shrugged and went back to the kitchen. "Maybe we'll go to Texas."

"Excuse me?"

"I think maybe it's time for me to go home."

"Good for you," I said. "But Colorado's *my* home! I don't want to go to Texas."

"We wouldn't stay there," she said. "We'd just go visit for a while, until we know what we're doing."

"Have you called them?"

"Who?"

"Your parents."

She put the mixing bowls on the counter and brushed her hair back from her forehead. "Not yet. But I know they'll love you."

"Those aren't ours," I said, nodding toward the mixing bowls.

"Are you sure?"

"They're the same ones everyone in the complex has."

"Oh." She put the bowls back.

I shook my head. She wasn't going to be able to pack any more than she was going to be able to plan for a future or pay her bills.

"Mom, slow down a minute. Let's just wait, okay?"

"Wait? Wait for what? I spent seventeen years waiting for Ales—for *him* to come back, and look what good it did me! I've had enough waiting. I'm never waiting again."

"But Mom—"

"No, Sandro. You were right. We should have left years ago."

"Can we at least wait till the end of school?" I wasn't sure why I said that, but as soon as I did, it gave me hope.

She looked at me. "Why?"

"Because it would be easier to finish the year here, without transferring credits and junk."

"I wish you had said something before I gave notice," she said irritably.

"You didn't give me a chance," I reminded her.

"Well, it's done," she said, turning around in the kitchen. "You'll just have to transfer. Why don't you go start packing your room?"

"What's the hurry? We're not leaving for a couple of weeks, right?"

"We don't want to put it off till the last minute," she said.

Deciding it was easier to just go to my room than to try to talk any sense into her, I picked up my backpack. "Just so you know, I put an ad in the *Save a Penny* for my skis," I said. "Hopefully, we'll be able to sell them before we go."

"Maybe you ought to keep them," she said, hesitantly.

"They won't do me any good in Texas."

"Keep the skis, Sandro," she said softly. "They may be the only thing—" She broke off and ran to the bathroom.

I shook my head. I had no idea what to do with her. She had always been flaky, but this was ridiculous. She wanted to move on from Alessandro, so she dumped her whole life, and mine, too. Then she wanted me to keep the skis to remind me of him?

Just as I was turning to shut my bedroom door, someone tried to get into our apartment. It happened a lot; people came home drunk and got the doors confused, so we always kept ours locked. When someone tried to get in, then, there was always an entertaining thud on the door, usually followed by either a "What the hell?" or other curse words.

This time, however, the first thud was followed by three brisk knocks, and then the sound of some fumbling. I dropped my backpack on the floor. "Wrong door," I called.

"Sandrino? Let me in."

I tried to swallow but didn't have enough spit to do it.

"Sandrino?" More knocking. "Unlock the door."

Mom came out of the bathroom, sniffling but otherwise composed. She took one look at me and said, "What's wrong?"

I didn't know how to answer, and fortunately, I didn't have to. "Please, Sandro. My hands are full!"

The color drained from my mom's face, but she moved faster than I did. She practically bounded across the room and yanked the door open. I was expecting her to knock Alessandro down with an enthusiastic hug.

She did knock him down, but it was with her fist.

In his defense, he never saw it coming. But it was still really impressive.

That one shot took it all out of her, though. She sank to her knees right there in the doorway. He sat up slowly, rubbing his cheek. "Tiffany?"

Mom didn't answer. She was crying too hard.

Alessandro was in the middle of several bags, packages, and roses. Apparently he had been holding a bouquet, and now the flowers were scattered all over. It looked like he had been carrying at least a dozen, maybe even two.

"Tiffany?" he said again, like he wasn't sure where he was. Frankly, I was impressed he was still conscious. "Tiffany, *amore*, what's wrong?"

Mom made a strangled sound and lurched to her feet. I thought she was going for Alessandro again, and apparently he did, too, because he raised both hands to block her.

Instead, Mom staggered back in and collapsed onto the couch. I was still just standing in my bedroom doorway, staring with my mouth hanging open.

Alessandro got to his feet, rather unsteadily, and picked up a couple of his bags. He started to come inside.

"What the hell do you think you're doing?"

He stopped with one foot in and one foot out. "I was . . . I thought . . . May I come in?"

"No!" Mom snapped. "Go back to whatever rock you crawled out from under!"

"Come on in," I said, walking into the living room.

"Sandro!" You would have thought I had stabbed her in the back.

"Mom, give him a break." Drawing nearer, I had noticed that he had a few days' growth, his eyes were bloodshot, and he looked beat. I reached out and took the bags from his hands. "Come on in," I repeated.

Mom stood up. "I'm leaving," she said stiffly.

Alessandro stopped, still in the doorway, looking confused. "Where are you going?"

"Nowhere," I said, glaring at Mom.

"Anywhere but here," she said, glaring right back. "I'm not staying if he is."

Sighing, I said, "I didn't say he was *staying*, Mom. I said he could *come in*. He came back. Shouldn't we give him a chance to explain?"

"I can't believe what you're saying!"

Neither could I, really, but I didn't see any point in admitting that.

Alessandro and I soon had all of his belongings inside and were able to close the front door. Then we sat in very awkward silence for several moments.

"Well?" Mom finally demanded.

Alessandro glanced at me and then looked at Mom. "I was hoping we could have a private reunion."

"There's not going to be a reunion, and anything you're going to say you can say to both of us." Mom wasn't making much sense, but at least she was talking to him.

He glanced at me again before turning to her. She glared at him the whole time, and didn't even stop when he knelt down before her.

"Tiffany, I love you."

"You show love by disappearing?" she demanded. "Where the hell were you?"

"I told you I was going home—" he started.

"No you didn't."

He blinked. "Yes, I did! The morning I left, I—" He broke off when he heard me groan.

"You told her while she was still in bed?" I asked.

"Well, yes, I—"

"Did you at least make her sit up?"

"No, I—"

"Well, that explains it all," I said, leaning against the wall and staring at my mother. She at least had the grace to blush a little.

"Explains what?" Alessandro asked, looking from me to Mom and back again.

"If you really knew Mom, you'd know that you can't expect her to remember anything you tell her before noon."

"What?"

"Never mind," Mom said, glaring at me. "What were you saying, Alessandro?" she asked. "What did you tell me before you left?"

"I did it. I sold everything."

"Alessandro!" Mom breathed.

"You sold everything?" I repeated. "What does that mean?"

Mom and Alessandro were staring at each other with an intensity that made me uncomfortable. "You sold your family's business?" she said.

He nodded. "And all the land."

"Oh, Alessandro!"

Things were shifting, faster than I was ready for. "Could you fill me in here?"

"Six months ago, before he died, my father received an offer for our business," Alessandro said to me while still looking at Mom. "I decided to take the offer. Unfortunately, the buyer and then my brother had some second thoughts, so it took longer than I thought it would."

Mom just stared at him.

"Didn't you get my flowers? I sent flowers."

I pulled the note from our neighbor out of my pocket and handed it to Mom. "You just sent them today."

"No, I ordered them last week."

"Was this the note on the front door?" Mom asked me.

"Yeah."

"It's says she's been holding these for a day or two," she said slowly. "We were never home when she was."

"And you couldn't call?" I asked him.

"Yes," Mom said. "Why didn't you call?"

"I wanted to surprise you," he said earnestly. "I thought it would only take three days at the most. When it took longer, I did try to call, several times. No one was ever home."

Mom looked sharply at me, and I realized that I had made a strange sound. I had just remembered unplugging the phone—again.

"Please, Tiffany, tell me why you're so mad!" Alessandro reached out tentatively and took her hand. "I gave up everything because I love you!"

"You left," Mom said, tearing up again.

"You left," I said in a much harsher tone. "You left, just like you did before." When he didn't say anything, I almost shouted, "Just like you did before! Don't you get it?"

"You thought I left you?" Alessandro said, reaching with his other hand and touching Mom's cheek. "How could you think that? I told you the night before how much I love you, how proud I am of Sandro, how much I want to be a part of your lives—"

"And then you left," Mom whispered.

Alessandro let go of Mom's hand and fumbled in his pocket for a second. Then he pulled out a small box. "Tiffany, will you marry me?"

Mom shrieked. I groaned.

"You're going to forgive him all over again, aren't you?"

Mom tore her eyes off Alessandro and looked at me with glowing happiness. "Yes. Because you showed me how."

I gaped at her for a second before I realized that she was right. I had forgiven him once, and I had actually opened the door for her to forgive him the second time. As much as I didn't want to believe it, I knew he was good for my mother.

I was literally saved by the bell when the phone rang. I went to answer it, happy to turn my back on my parents as they fell into each other's arms.

"Hi, Angela," I said.

"How'd you know it was me?"

"The stars told me you'd call," I said, looking out the window and impulsively wishing on one.

"I thought that you thought fate is a lot of crap," she teased.

"It is," I said. *Maybe.*

EPILOGUE

- - -

The wand was resting lightly against my boots, but the countdown tones hadn't started yet. I adjusted my grip on my poles and took a couple of deep breaths.

From up here, I couldn't hear the sounds of the crowd that would be cheering by the time I reached the bottom of the run. Mom, Alessandro, and Angela were all waiting for me, along with the rest of the family and friends at the State Championship Ski Meet.

At the first tone, I smiled. The mountain was waiting for my skis, and I was ready to follow them to my destiny, wherever that turned out to be.

S.L. Rottman, a former English teacher who grew up spending time in a Colorado ski town, is the author of six novels for teenagers, including the award-winning *Hero*, *Rough Waters*, and *Stetson*.